RIVER ODYSSEY

OTHER BOOKS BY
PHILIP ROY

Submarine Outlaw

Journey to Atlantis

River
Odyssey

PHILIP ROY

RONSDALE PRESS

RONSDALE PRESS
3350 West 21st Avenue, Vancouver, B.C., Canada V6S 1G7
www.ronsdalepress.com

Typesetting: Julie Cochrane, in Minion 12 pt on 16
Cover Art & Design: Massive Graphic
Paper: Ancient Forest Friendly "Silva" (FSC) — 100% post-consumer waste,
    totally chlorine-free and acid-free

Ronsdale Press wishes to thank the following for their support of its publishing program: the Canada Council for the Arts, the Government of Canada through the Canada Book Program, the British Columbia Arts Council and the Province of British Columbia through the British Columbia Book Publishing Tax Credit program.

Library and Archives Canada Cataloguing in Publication

Roy, Philip, 1960–
    River odyssey / Philip Roy.

(The submarine outlaw series; 3)
ISBN 978-1-55380-105-4

    I. Title. II. Series: Roy, Philip, 1960–. Submarine outlaw series; 3.

PS8635.O91144R58 2010   jC813'.6   C2010-904863-6

At Ronsdale Press we are committed to protecting the environment. To this end we are working with Canopy (formerly Markets Initiative) and printers to phase out our use of paper produced from ancient forests. This book is one step towards that goal.

Printed in Canada by Marquis Printing, Quebec

for Julia

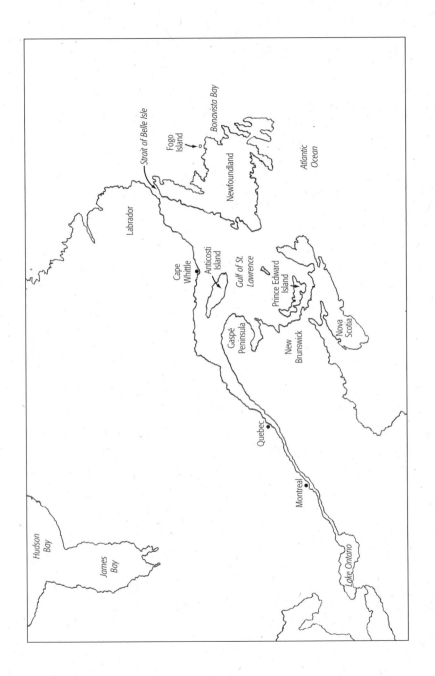

Chapter 1

IT BEGAN WITH a conversation.

I was sitting on the floor of Sheba's cottage. I had books, maps and charts open everywhere. There was a cockatiel on my shoulder, a cat on my lap, a dozen dogs and cats on the floor and sofa behind me, a tortoise slowly creeping under one book and a goat wanting to eat another. I was preparing for my longest journey yet, to the great Pacific Ocean, when Sheba appeared in the doorway from the kitchen. She was wearing a white dress with tiny green, yellow and pink flowers speckled over it. Her hair fell in red shell-like tresses all the way down the front of her dress like two rivers of red gold. In the spring Sheba dressed like the May Queen.

"Alfred!"

I looked up. Sheba was the voice of love for all creatures, living and otherwise. She was also the voice of omens, good and bad, and it was wise to listen to her. In the ancient world they would have called her an oracle.

"Yes?"

She threw her next words at me like a quest. "You must find your father!"

"What?"

The cockatiel flew to the top of the bookcase. The tortoise stuck his head out from underneath the atlas, then pulled it back in. Sheba returned to the kitchen.

I was so stunned I didn't know what to think. I got up, brushed the cat fur from my lap and went to the kitchen. Hollie was curled up on a mat by the door, ready in case I should go outside. Edgar, the kitchen goat, was standing by the stove looking as if somebody had just died, though he always looked that way. Sheba had returned to sit at the table, had thrown on her apron and was peeling onions and garlic. She was peeling slowly and her eyes were watered with tears.

"I'm getting ready to go to the Pacific."

"I know, Alfred."

"I've never even seen my father."

"I know."

"He . . . he left when my mother died, when I was born."

Sheba looked up with a loving smile beneath onion tears.

Her eyes were green like a cat's and sparkled when they were wet. "I know, Alfred."

I sat down. She was filling two bowls with garlic and onion bulbs. Her garlic was big and her onions were small. Both had been grown and picked right here in the kitchen, Sheba's hydroponic garden, where it was always summer. Outside, the fog rolled up against the windows. Ziegfried said that Sheba could grow a tomato from a stone. I believed it. I sat and watched her peel, and waited. My two favourite places in the world were Sheba's kitchen and my submarine.

"I dreamt about you last night," she said finally.

Now I knew I was in for it. If Sheba dreamt about you, you were in for it.

"There was a big storm," she began.

I sat up and listened closely. A big storm was no big deal; I had seen lots of those.

"And there was a sea monster."

Not so good. "What did it look like?"

"I couldn't see it; I just knew it was there. And your submarine was sinking."

Shoot! "Was the monster pulling it down?"

"Yes, I think so. I'm not sure. It's just that . . ."

"What?"

"Well . . ."

"What? What is it?"

"I think maybe the sea monster was your father."

"My *father*? How could it be my father? And why would

he want to sink my submarine? He doesn't even know me."

"I know, Alfred. I don't know why. It was him and it wasn't him."

I didn't like where this was going.

"There was an angel too."

"An angel? What did it look like? Did you see it?"

"No. I was waking. She just called out, 'Alfred!'"

Sheba's eyes drifted onto the onion she was peeling but I could guess where her mind was. She was twelve the last time she had seen her own father. She turned and looked at me.

"And then she said, 'Forgive.' But I don't know if she meant you were supposed to forgive someone else, or ask for forgiveness for yourself."

"Which one do you think it was?"

"I don't know."

"And you didn't see what she looked like?"

"No."

"What did she sound like?"

"Kind."

"Why would I have to ask for forgiveness? What did *I* do?"

"I don't know. Maybe that's not what she meant. Maybe you're supposed to forgive somebody else."

"Who? My father?"

"Perhaps. The important thing is that you find him. Then you will know."

"But why?"

"I don't know, Alfred, but I don't dream about angels and sea monsters every night. It is an important dream."

I didn't like to argue with Sheba. I wasn't really arguing with her, I was just trying to understand.

"But I'm happy."

"You're happy now."

"Yes."

"But this dream tells me that something is coming your way. And you need to find out what it is. You can either go out and meet it, or wait until it finds you, but something tells me you'll be happier if you find it first."

"My father?"

"Maybe. Maybe something else."

"Like what?"

"I don't know."

I watched as Edgar dropped his head onto Sheba's shoulder and waited for her to scratch him. Even as she did, he looked like the world had just ended. That was his nature. He was a goat.

I had no intention of going looking for my father.

That night I crawled into my sleeping bag on the floor by the bay window. Hollie dug a trench between my feet and made himself as comfortable as a little dog could considering he was dwarfed by all the other dogs and most of the cats. During the night a few more warm bodies settled onto the bag, making turning difficult. I couldn't sleep anyway.

The night time was always when my worst thoughts came. That's what I liked about the sub; we sailed at night and slept during the day.

I didn't want to search for my father. Why should I, when he obviously didn't want to find me? If he had, he would have. But he never did. If I went looking for him and found him, wherever he was, he probably wouldn't appreciate it very much. He probably wouldn't like me. In fact, maybe he would hate me. Why should I go looking for somebody who might hate me?

But a thought was nagging me. What if my father had *wanted* to find me but couldn't? What if he was sick or handicapped in some way and was lying in a bed all these years hoping to see his only son? How terrible would that be? No. That was silly. I only thought like that at night when I couldn't sleep. My father was just busy living his own life somewhere else and never even thought about me and probably didn't even remember that he had a son in the first place.

I needed to roll over in my sleeping bag but didn't want to disturb the animals so I pulled my legs up slowly, turned and slid them back in. I took a deep breath and sighed. Then I felt a tug at my shoulder. I opened my eyes. It was Sheba. In her gentle, songlike voice, as if it were the most natural thing in the world, she alerted me: "Alfred. There's a ghost on the point."

I jumped to my feet. I had been waiting for this for two years. Sheba's sightings of ghosts, mermaids, flaming ships and strange creatures from the sea, which I had never seen myself, at least not clearly, yet hated to discredit because I respected her so much, had fascinated me ever since the day we met. Was I finally going to see a ghost for myself?

I dressed as quickly as I could and joined her in the kitchen. She said we had to go without a light and leave all the animals in the house. We didn't want to spook the ghost.

"They're very nervous," she explained as we shut the kitchen door and tip-toed down the path towards the point. "It won't stay long."

I was nervous myself. Were we really about to see a ghost?

"How did you know there was one here?" I asked.

"I can just tell. It's a feeling. It wakes me up."

Sheba's island was probably one of the tiniest in all of Newfoundland. It rose only fifty feet above the tide at its highest point and had a circumference only a little bigger than a soccer field. But her cottage was well protected by rock and its foundation had recently been fortified by Ziegfried. The "point" was the most easterly corner of the island, where the rocks dropped like steps into the sea. Sheba said it was a favourite stopping spot for seals, seabirds, mermaids and ghosts.

I followed her down the path. The fog had mostly lifted. It was a good thing I was walking with her and didn't just stumble into her, because, being a whole head taller than me, with her long flowing hair and flowing skirts, and the forward-leaning gait she had when she walked, she'd be kind of scary to run into in the dark.

We came around a corner of the rock and she grabbed my elbow. I stopped.

"There!" she said in a whisper.

I looked. And I saw it!

The ghost was smaller than me. At first, I thought it was just a ball of light, like a reflection of a whole bunch of fragments of light in a mist, but the longer I stared, the more I saw that it had the shape of a man. I didn't see arms or a face but it stood with the posture of a person, as if it were deep in thought. My foot made a sound on the rocks and the figure turned. It appeared to be looking at us and that frightened me. Who knew what a ghost would do?

"Don't go," Sheba said softly.

She wasn't speaking to me. The ghost bent down over the edge of the water. Was it injured? I wanted to ask Sheba if she thought it was injured but she held her finger in front of her mouth. The ghost was shaking. Was it hurt? Was it crying? I turned to Sheba and saw a tear run down her cheek. I looked at the ghost. It was just a ball of light, really, and yet it looked so much like it was crying. I turned to Sheba again; her eyes welled up with tears. When I looked back, the ghost was gone. I never saw it enter the water. I never saw it leave at all. It was there one moment, gone the next. I felt a lump in my throat. The air was so heavy.

"Will it come back?" I asked.

"No," Sheba said. "Not tonight."

Chapter 2

THE FLOOR SHOOK beneath my head and I knew that Ziegfried had arrived. He must have driven his truck through the night and taken the motorboat across from the mainland as the sun was coming up. Either that or I had slept in. The next thing I needed to know was whether I had just dreamt I saw a ghost or had really seen one. I remembered the figure crying over the water like a lost soul at the very edge of the world.

No. It hadn't been a dream.

I dressed, rolled up my bag and went to the kitchen. Ziegfried was standing there as tall as a giant, his eyes wide—the look he got when he knew something had happened but didn't want to talk about it in front of Sheba. She must have told him something already. Sheba was the sparkle in Ziegfried's life. He believed she was the reason he had been put on this earth—for her, and to fix things, fiddle with things and invent things. Even so, I knew he would prefer to question me about ghosts when we were alone.

He hung up his jacket, washed his hands and sat at the table. He always brought the smell of outdoors in with him: the smell of wood, oil, metal and earth, a little like a bear. The animals shifted nervously when he came in, even though in Sheba's world the animals were treated like people. The cockatiels flew to his head and chirped loudly, to show they were not afraid, although Ziegfried kept a house full of birds himself, and a bird knows a bird's friend. All the same, when he reached over to pat Edgar's head, the goat twitched nervously and seemed about half the size he was before. All the animals must have felt they were in the presence of a giant.

"How's the sub, Al?"

"Perfect."

"Good. The engine?"

"Singing."

"Good. Your wake?"

"True as an arrow."

"Good. Good."

Ziegfried wrapped his hands around a cup of tea Sheba poured for him. As we sat down to breakfast she described her dream and what she thought I should do. He listened carefully and stole occasional glances at me. He knew I was geared up for the Pacific; we had prepared for it all winter. Still, I didn't think he would ever contradict Sheba. But he surprised me.

"Well, I haven't got much to say for a man who didn't care enough to stay around after you came into the world."

I raised my head. Sheba didn't seem the least bit disturbed.

"Has he ever written to you, Al?" he continued.

"No."

"Not a birthday present, not a Christmas card, ever?"

"No. Nothing."

Ziegfried raised his bushy eyebrows. "What father doesn't send even one letter to his own son?"

"Maybe a father who has made a mistake," said Sheba. She spoke so gently it was as if she were speaking from another world. "Maybe a father who is ashamed. Or a man who has been deeply hurt." She looked into my eyes. "*Everyone* makes mistakes."

"That's true," Ziegfried agreed quickly.

I wondered what mistakes he ever made.

"It is unfinished business," Sheba said. "Like the ghost who visited us last night. The poor thing died with unfinished business. Now it roams the world like a shadow."

I watched Ziegfried's face to see if he believed what she had just said. He listened to every word that came from her lips as if it were the gospel truth.

"You need to find your father, Alfred," Sheba continued.

"It doesn't matter if you like him or not. It doesn't matter if he likes you or not. You need to meet him, face to face, and speak with him. Then you will know what to do. Then you can let him go if you want to. Then it won't haunt you."

"It doesn't haunt me. He's not a ghost."

"Not yet," she said, with a certainty that cut right through both of us. You can't argue with someone who is motivated only by love.

Ziegfried furrowed his brow. "Have you got any idea where he might be, Al?"

"My grandfather said he moved to Montreal and got a job there in the dockyards. He's a machinist."

"Montreal?"

"Yah, but that was a long time ago."

"Sixteen years ago."

"I guess so."

Ziegfried shook his head. "Seems to me he's not worth the trouble."

"Maybe he isn't," said Sheba, and her eyes sparkled, "but Alfred is."

"Sheba has a kind of intelligence you and I don't have," said Ziegfried. "If it were anybody else, talking about angels and ghosts . . ."

We had stepped out to carry in supplies from the motorboat. He had moored it to the sub, which was moored to the rock in Sheba's tiny cove.

"*You've* seen ghosts before," I said.

"Nope. Never have."

"What? But you told me you did, a couple of years ago."

"No, Al. What I said was that I *believed* in ghosts. I never said I saw one."

"Oh. Then why do you believe in them if you've never seen one?"

"Because so many people have. If you hear enough people talk about something, you kind of start to believe it yourself. I've never seen Australia but I believe it exists."

"Oh."

"What did you see, Al, a bright light?"

"Yah. It was a bright light. But it was something else too."

"Really? What?"

I thought for a while. "It had . . . personality."

"Personality? The ghost had personality?"

"I don't know how else to describe it."

"Did you see a face?"

"No."

"Did you see clothes, or tools?"

"No. Nothing. It was just . . . its posture."

"Its posture?"

"Yah. The way it was standing."

"Did you see its legs?"

"No."

"Its arms?"

"No. Nothing."

"But you knew it was standing?"

"Yes. And then it bent over, and then it was gone. It was sad. *Really* sad."

Ziegfried scratched his head.

"You should ask Sheba about it. She saw it too."

"No, no, heavens, no! No, that's enough. If you say you saw it, then I know it was there. You're like me, Al, scientific minded. If you say you saw a ghost, then I believe you saw a ghost."

I knew that would not be the end of it for him. In the afternoon, while Sheba was practising yoga in her room, I saw him scouting around on the point. He had his measuring tape out and was making sketches in his notepad. I had to smile. If a ghost like that was afraid of someone my size, Ziegfried was sure as heck never going to see one.

Everything was mixed up now and I hated that. I wanted to sail to the Pacific, not search for my father. But I didn't want to disappoint Sheba, and she thought I should search for him. Disappointing Sheba would have bothered me more than anything else. But maybe I could convince her that I didn't need to look for him, and things could straighten out again and we could continue preparing for the Pacific.

I wandered around mulling it over in my head until I found myself in front of her bedroom door. I hated to disturb her when she was practising yoga, but couldn't help it; it was bugging me so much. I knocked.

"Yes?"

"Can I talk to you?"

"Come in."

I opened the door. She was on a mat on the floor. Her arms and legs were twisted up like very smooth licorice. She moved slowly, limb over limb like a snake. Her hair fell down and covered her feet. She waited for me to speak.

"I'm sorry to bother you."

"You're not bothering me."

"Umm . . . I don't think I should look for my father."

She raised her head, but not towards me. She looked like a turtle now, extending its head out of its shell. "I do."

Shoot. I just wished she would give up. "I think I know why you think I should go."

She stopped moving, turned and looked at me. "Why?"

"Because you were only twelve the last time you saw your own father."

I hoped my words wouldn't hurt her. I didn't want to hurt her. Maybe they did. She reached her arms towards me. "Come here."

I went over and sat down. She took my hands in hers and stared into my eyes. "Yes. It was the last time I saw him, Alfred. But there is something else you must know. Something I am ashamed to tell you. Something I think of every day of my life. How I wish I could go back and change it. I would do anything if I could. But I can't."

"What is it?"

"I had another chance to see him."

"Who? Your father?"

"Yes. When I was fifteen. Some friends of mine were having a party. They weren't really my friends; they were older than me and I wanted to be their friend. They had never invited me to a party before. I wanted to go so much. But my father was sick then. He sent a message that he wanted to see me. I should have gone. I could have taken a train to the town where he lived. I should have gone to see him. He asked for me."

"But you didn't?"

Her eyes fell onto the floor.

"No. I went to the party. My father died the next day. I wasn't there. He died without me. He must have thought I didn't care. I was just a silly fifteen-year-old girl who wanted to be popular. If I could change just one thing, Alfred, it would be that. How could I have been so selfish? What does a party mean when your father is dying?"

I didn't know what to say.

"A time will come, Alfred, when you will be older than your father was when he left you. You will be wiser then than he was. You are probably wiser now. I promise you, a time will come when you will wish you had made the effort to see him. Perhaps he is too afraid to come seeking you. Perhaps he is not strong enough. But you are strong enough, and you are brave. You can go to him. If you choose not to now, later might be too late. I would spare you that if I could. Do you know that I love you?"

"Yes."

Sheba's eyes were filled with tears but she was smiling. I dropped my head and nodded. She was right. I wished she wasn't but she was. "I'm sorry I interrupted you."

She squeezed my hands again. "I'm glad that you did."

I went down to the cove and threw the Frisbee with Hollie and Seaweed and thought it over. Throwing the Frisbee with a dog and seagull wasn't easy. I would spin it over the water with all my might and Seaweed would fly over and pick it up. Then, he would fly to the sub, hover in the air above it and drop the Frisbee inside the portal. Sometimes it would go in but usually it would bounce off the hatch and land in the water. That's when Hollie would jump in and retrieve it, which was a lot of work for him because he was no bigger than the Frisbee. And he wouldn't give it to me unless I traded him something for it, like a stick or a dog biscuit. But sometimes Seaweed would suddenly lose interest and Hollie and I would have to climb into the motorboat and go out and get the Frisbee back. And sometimes, in the fog, we couldn't find it. Still, it was better than playing alone.

"What do you think, Hollie? Do you want to sail to Montreal?"

Hollie wagged his tail and barked excitedly. He wanted to go everywhere.

"How about you, Seaweed?"

Seaweed turned his beak sideways, giving his questioning

look. That was all I was going to get out of him. But I knew the truth already: both would follow me anywhere without question or complaint. They were the most loyal crew in the world.

By suppertime I had decided. When I told Ziegfried and Sheba that I was going to search for my father they listened quietly and didn't say anything for a while, although Sheba threw me an approving look. When Ziegfried finally spoke, he revealed that he had anticipated my decision. He had already turned his genius towards the task.

"It's just six hundred miles, Al, from the mouth of the St. Lawrence to Montreal. The river flows a maximum of seven knots with the retreating tide. I figure it will take you a month tops. A week or so upstream, you do what you have to do, and a week back. Then, we stock for the Pacific. A month tops, Al."

My mouth dropped. "Sail up the St. Lawrence River?"

"Sure. Why not? Freighters do it every day."

Wow. It had never crossed my mind to sail my submarine up a river. Could we sail into the heart of a city like Montreal, just like that? What about the people everywhere? What about the river traffic? Where would we hide the sub? My mind raced through the potential obstacles: river currents, shallow water, ocean freighters in narrow channels, bustling cities. Where would we sleep? How would we avoid being seen? It seemed like a heck of a challenge to me.

Cool.

Chapter 3

ZIEGFRIED SAID IT was "ironic" I had left school at fourteen and had been studying ever since. I never really thought about it. All I knew was that you couldn't go to sea, stay safe, not get lost and find anything interesting at all if you didn't read about it first. That was just common sense. And then, once you decided to go somewhere, every scrap of information you got your hands on became important and interesting. I never knew, for instance, that the tide could travel hundreds of miles up a river. And it did a lot more than that; it brought seals, dolphins, whales, ocean-liners, freighters and submarines with it. I discovered that in the first book I pulled from Sheba's bookshelf, *Rivers of the World*.

Sheba kept books all over the house. She was a compulsive reader. Every month she ordered them from a store in St. John's that brought them in from around the world. Her favourite topics were ecology, anthropology, geography, mysticism and religion. She also ordered books on spells, mushrooms, flowers and other growing things, but these books never made it out of the kitchen, and Ziegfried and I were kind of afraid to touch them. When she saw me standing by the shelf, she came over, reached up for a small book and handed it to me.

"What's this?"

"*Jacques Cartier.*"

"Oh."

"Do you know how old Cartier was when he went to sea?" she asked with her song-like voice.

"How old?"

"Thirteen."

"Oh."

I tucked the book under my arm. I was fourteen when I went to sea.

The next day, Ziegfried and I carried water, fruit, canned food and fuel down to the sub. Sheba was busy in the kitchen baking cookies, bread and pizza—fresh food for the trip. Travelling in a submarine wasn't very expensive when there was just one of you and your crew was a dog and seagull. The biggest cost was diesel fuel, but diesel goes a long way in a streamlined vessel with an efficient motor. I had eight thousand dollars left from my share of the treasure I had found in Louisbourg harbour on our first voyage. We sold the gold coins to a private collector for eighteen thousand dollars and split it fifty-fifty. Ziegfried wanted me to keep it all but I refused. Sheba said I should start taking photographs on my journeys and keep a journal so that I could sell stories to travel and geographic magazines. It could be a way to pay for future explorations. That sounded like a good idea to me.

Over the winter we had constructed solar panels and a wind turbine for the sub, two exciting new sources of power designed specifically for sailing in the Pacific, where the sun was strong and distances far. But we hadn't tested them yet and would wait until the river voyage was over. When they were installed, the sub would have five distinct sources of power: diesel engine, electric battery, stationary bicycle, solar panels and a wind turbine. Ziegfried had designed all of the systems and I helped him build them. When the sub was out of water Ziegfried was absolute boss. He was master-designer and I was just his assistant. I was alternately cutting, filing, sanding, polishing metal, glass and wood, endlessly splicing wire, and cleaning up. Ziegfried made every decision concerning the construction and safety of the sub, including when she would go back in the water. No one could change his mind about that even a tiny bit, no one. Once the sub was in the water, however, I became her captain again and I was in charge. Only I decided where and when she sailed. It was a strange shift of roles but it happened naturally and it worked well.

Ziegfried lowered the provisions into the sub and I stashed them into the corners and hung them from the rafters, spreading them as evenly as possible. While we worked, I asked him if he had discovered anything interesting when he was scouting on the point. He raised his head as if he had been expecting me to ask.

"I did, in fact."

"Really? What?"

He looked at me with an awkward smile. It wasn't something he would like to say in front of Sheba.

"Iron."

"Iron? What do you mean?"

"In the rock. There's an unusually large quantity of iron in some of the rocks."

"So?"

"Well . . ."

"What?"

He took a deep breath. "If you have one rock that's mostly iron and another that's mostly sandstone, and the sun heats them both up, then, the sun goes down . . ."

"Yes?"

"Well, the rocks are going to cool down at different rates."

"Okay. So?"

"Well, if you have mist in the air to catch and reflect light, such as the light of the moon and stars, or a passing ship, then that patch of unstable air above the rocks could potentially trap the light and create a light phenomenon."

"Oh. You mean . . . it might *look* like a ghost."

"Well, yes, it could, if what you saw was just light."

"Oh."

"That's the theory anyway. But I don't think Sheba is very interested in theories, do you?"

"No. I don't think so."

Ziegfried always had a logical explanation for things.

"But how would you explain that the light had personality, that it looked sad?"

"I have no doubt that that is what you felt, Al, but your feelings were a reaction to what you saw, truth be told. You must learn to separate your feelings from the object under investigation; otherwise you might be tempted to say that a butterfly is happy and a frog is bored."

"Oh."

It wasn't the first time I found myself somewhere between Ziegfried's brilliant, logical mind and Sheba's magical, instinctual understanding, but it was probably the first time I found Sheba's view more convincing. After all, how could he explain the fact that she had been woken by the ghost in the middle of the night? And besides, I had seen it for myself, and it looked like more than light to me.

We went to sea the next day. We never had time to send for proper charts. No matter, I thought, we had detailed maps of the river, with soundings marked in fathoms. And we had sonar. We ought to be fine with those. We did have charts for the Strait of Belle Isle and the water around Anticosti Island.

In the twilight I untied the ropes, climbed into the sub and flipped the engine switch. The engine purred softly, like a sleeping goat. Its vibration came up through the floor as the sub rocked gently from side to side. Seaweed and Hollie took their places by the observation window in the floor of the bow. We were supposed to be going to the Pacific, I knew, but that journey would have to wait.

Sheba and Ziegfried saw us off with hugs but no tears. We'd be back soon enough. It was just a short journey to Montreal. I would find my father, say whatever needed to be said, and sail back. Yet Sheba wore a serious expression on her face. She had read my cards after supper. "Something terrible is going to happen," she said. "But you will be all right. And you will return richer than before."

"A month tops, Al," said Ziegfried, then gave me one of his crushing bear hugs.

I stood in the portal and saluted them both as we motored out of the tiny cove. They stood and waved. They looked like giants to me.

Chapter 4

WE SAILED NORTH out of Bonavista Bay, around the Fogo Islands and westward towards Dark Cove, my home. I had never met my grandfather on the water before but that was the most practical thing to do and he would respect that. I wanted to ask him where I might find my father. I knew he would be out in the early morning; I just hoped he would be alone in his boat.

He was.

I kept the hull underwater anyway as I approached, leaving only two feet of the portal showing. I didn't want other fishermen to spot the sub. Only my grandparents and Sheba knew where it was from. The coastguard would take it from me if they ever caught me. They would want to inspect it and that would take forever and likely I would never get it back. Nor did I have any kind of captain's or pilot's license. I was an outlaw by the laws of the land.

He looked lonely in the boat pulling traps by himself. If I hadn't gone to sea as an explorer that's exactly where I would be right now, standing beside him like his shadow, working silently all day because my grandfather never spoke on the boat when he was working.

He seemed surprisingly happy to see me. He stood up with his hands on his hips and smiled as we approached. I didn't think I had ever seen him smile before. It made him look younger.

"Well, look at this!"

"Hi, Grandpa!"

"Aren't *you* as quiet as a ghost on the water; I never heard you coming."

"I was careful of the lines."

He nodded. He was still smiling.

"Heading to Australia, are you?"

"Not yet. I'm sailing to Montreal first."

"*Montreal?* Are you going to go in that thing?"

"Yup."

"Well . . . I suppose you could. But why on earth do you want to go to Montreal?"

"Uhhhh . . . I figured I might have a look around for my father."

The smile washed off my grandfather's face. "Oh, well, now there's a waste of a trip. Nothing good's going to come of that."

I felt the same way. I just didn't want to tell him that.

"Sheba says it's unfinished business."

"Unfinished business? Yes, well, I suppose it is that, isn't it?"

"Do you think I'd find him on the dockyards probably?"

"More than likely. He wasn't one to move around much once he settled. Wasn't like you. Unfinished business is it? Seems to me you're going to open a can of worms there, Alfred. He's not like you, you know. Better be straight about that before you start."

I didn't really want to ask the next question. It just kind of jumped out.

"What was he like?"

My grandfather dropped his head to think. I waited for his answer, wishing I hadn't asked.

"He's not like you."

Fair enough. I wasn't expecting him to be like me anyway. And if my grandfather had bad things to say about my father, I didn't want to hear them either. I didn't even *want* to go looking for him; I was just following Sheba's advice, and it probably wasn't a good idea in the first place. Maybe stopping by to see my grandfather wasn't a good idea either. I just wanted to get to Montreal, get it over with, get back and prepare for the Pacific. What a waste of time.

After we said goodbye I sailed an hour west of Dark Cove, submerged to a hundred feet, shut everything off, turned the lights low and climbed into bed. Seaweed had flown to shore to mingle with the local birds. He was a sociable bird. Hollie made himself cozy on his blanket and I heard him chew his rubber ball, lick his paws, bite his tail, wrestle with his rope, lick his paws again and sigh. Only then did I fall asleep.

Ten hours later I woke and stretched. Hollie stretched too. I put the kettle on for tea, rose to the surface, opened the hatch and waited for Seaweed. It was misty in the twilight and the sub was invisible from shore, even for a seagull. But Seaweed would remember exactly where we had gone down. He had an amazing ability to find us, no matter what. Most often when we surfaced he was already on the hull before I opened the hatch. And sometimes, like tonight, he returned with friends—a couple of tough-looking seagulls. Were they expecting to stay? I sure hoped not. Nope. When I started the engine, the gulls flew off into the mist.

"Hi, Seaweed. Want some breakfast?"

As twilight faded into darkness we sailed out of Notre Dame Bay and headed north to sail around the Northern Peninsula into the Strait of Belle Isle. The sub plowed through the waves like a small whale. I sat at the controls, drank my tea and read Sheba's book. I was surprised to discover that Jacques Cartier had sailed this way. His first voyage, in 1534, had taken him across the Atlantic in only twenty days. That was incredible. He had only a sailing ship. He had only the wind. How could he do it in twenty days? It had taken us a week and a half to cross the Atlantic a year ago, and we had a powerful diesel engine, although we had stopped in the Azores along the way. Cartier would have been at the mercy of the winds. The winds at sea were like monsters that were always changing their minds. They might blow you straight for a day or so, spin you around and around like a bug in a tea cup, then blow you back to where you came from. His third voyage took three months. That seemed more realistic but must have been awful. And why would he bother to sail all the way around Newfoundland and down the Strait of Belle Isle anyway? That didn't make sense. Oh . . . he never knew there was open water between Newfoundland and Nova Scotia. It hadn't been discovered yet. I read that on the next page. Cartier was looking for a shortcut to China, and he thought he was close. Boy was *he* wrong.

He must have been pretty tough though. People in those days believed in sea monsters. They drew them on their maps. Some believed you could sail right over the edge of the world and fall into nothingness! How scary was that?

It was a very short night. The sun was up and on our backs long before we entered the Strait of Belle Isle. I tried to keep an equal distance between the Northern Peninsula and the coast of Labrador as we turned to port and headed southwest. I didn't want anyone to spot us with their telescopes. There were lots of people it seemed to me, with nothing better to do than stare at sea all day with a telescope.

And if they spotted something, especially a submarine, they just couldn't get on the phone fast enough. No need to tell everyone where we were sailing, I figured. Perhaps if we stayed out of sight long enough people would forget we were still around. Then we could explore more freely.

Radar showed a vessel ahead of us in the strait. I poked my head out of the portal and saw a ship. I didn't even need binoculars. She was huge! I could see traces of her wake still. Wow! I wondered if she were going to Montreal. Could such a ship sail up the river? Cartier's first ship was only fifty feet long. That was two and a half times longer than the sub. And it carried thirty men! Next to the ship ahead of us Cartier's ship would have looked like a minnow beside a whale.

She would know by radar that we were behind her, following her, though she would never have been able to see us. I wanted to close the distance. I wanted to take a closer look at her, but she was sailing at a very decent speed, almost twenty knots. That was impressive. We could only catch her if we stayed on the surface with the engine cranked all the way up, and that would take a few hours. Submerged we didn't stand a chance. What would they think if we snuck up behind her? Would they report a submarine to the coast-guard? If they did, we could dive and disappear. That's what submarines were good at—disappearing. I decided to stay on the surface and close our distance to a few miles. I really wanted to take a closer look at her. I didn't know why but I had a funny feeling about this ship.

Chapter 5

WE FOLLOWED THE freighter into the mouth of the St. Lawrence. She was stacked with containers, one on top of another like blocks in a pyramid, and for some reason reminded me of the Incredible Hulk. If the wind picked up, I was sure she was going to topple over. I thought maybe she was going to continue south towards New Brunswick, or Prince Edward Island, but as soon as she passed Cape Whittle she made a sharp turn to starboard. It looked strangely like a last minute decision. I had a sudden thought, too, that maybe I could just *say* we had sailed to Montreal, and not really go. We could sail around the Maritimes, maybe visit Sable Island again and see the ponies this time. Of course I

would never do that—lie to Sheba and Ziegfried. But thinking about it made me realize just how much I didn't want
to go to Montreal. As the sun dropped behind the hills of
Quebec, I turned to starboard and followed the hulking
freighter into the mouth of the river.

The St. Lawrence is not the longest river in the world. The
Nile is. And the Amazon is the biggest river in the world by
volume. It is bigger than all the next eight largest rivers com-
bined. It is so powerful that, two hundred miles from its
mouth, out at sea, you can still taste fresh water. I read that in
Sheba's book, *Rivers of the World*. But the St. Lawrence does
have something that's the biggest in the world: its mouth.

The mouth of the river is so big it never felt as though we
were leaving the sea at all. And when I reached down and
scooped a mouthful of water to taste, it was just as salty as
the sea. It didn't seem that the river was pouring into the
sea so much as the sea was pouring into the river. And it
was, all the way to Montreal.

I carried Hollie up so we could stand in the portal and
feel the wind in our faces. He raised his nose and sniffed.
He could smell land. The whiskers of his eyebrows were
growing over his eyes, making him blink.

"Hollie. I have to cut your eyebrows."

He looked up at me as if he were trying to make up his
mind.

"I do. You're starting to look like an old man."

Actually, he looked more like a seal. He was such a sea dog.

Anticosti Island lay straight ahead. I figured we could reach it by midnight, though I had been up twenty-four hours already. Usually we'd be sleeping now, and it was not our habit to ride on the surface in broad daylight. But we were in the mouth of a river, not the open Atlantic. Surely we wouldn't run into coastguard ships here?

I watched the radar closely. Radar is like magic. It is an electronic, all-seeing eye for ten miles. If there were a tin can in the water ten miles away we might pick it up on radar. But if there were a thousand steel-hulled ships eleven miles away, we wouldn't even know they were there. The moment they sailed into that magical ten-mile diameter, however, they would show up as blinking green dots on our radar screen. The hulking freighter was four miles ahead and she glowed like a fat bug on the screen.

I closed our distance to three miles, then two, then one-and-a-half. That was close enough. Even from a mile and a half away the wake of the ship flattened the waves in front of the sub. I stood in the portal with the binoculars and scanned her stern. The containers were stacked tightly like a wall of giant, gray-brown Lego. It amazed me that such a monstrosity could even float, yet here she was cutting twenty knots through the water. And then, I saw something weird.

Out of the corner of one of the highest containers crawled three men. They emerged as if from a hole in a wall. They shielded their eyes from the sun and staggered as they reached for places to cling to the back of the container.

Stowaways! I wished I could have seen them more clearly. They seemed pretty weak and shaky and one of them almost fell overboard, but the others grabbed him in time. He was lucky. It would have been a deadly fall. Then, just as suddenly as they appeared, they disappeared. For a second it crossed my mind that they might be ghosts, but just for a second. It was more likely they had crawled back inside the hole they had come out of. Things have a way of distorting through binoculars from a distance. One of the men scrambled out again but an arm reached out, grabbed him and pulled him back in. They were definitely not ghosts.

I heard the radar beep and two lights jumped onto the screen. Two vessels were coming from the south and were moving fast. Judging from their speed they must have been speedboats. I stood at the screen for a moment and watched as the radar sweep tracked their progress. They were coming directly for the freighter and were travelling at least forty knots. At that speed it would take them less than ten minutes to reach their goal. It was time for us to leave.

Curiosity killed the cat, my grandmother used to say. I couldn't help it. I wanted to know who was coming so fast before we submerged. They had to be speedboats; that much I knew. Nothing else could travel so fast on the surface except hydrofoils, and there were no hydrofoils in the Maritimes that I had ever heard of. Perhaps they were recreational speedboats. But why would they intercept a freighter? Had they picked her up on radar and were just curious, like me? No, that didn't make sense. They must have known there were stowaways on board. But how could they know that? Had the stowaways been spotted in the Strait of Belle Isle? I bet that was it. I bet the people with telescopes pointed out at sea, who made a hobby of watching passing ships to see where they were coming from and what they were carrying, had spotted them and alerted the authorities. If I could see them from a-mile-and-a-half away through binoculars, someone with a powerful telescope would have no trouble spotting them from shore. That must have been it. That made sense.

But I still wanted to know who was coming, so I strapped on the harness, climbed on top of the portal, stood up and stared through the binoculars. Two dark spots appeared on the horizon from the south. They were spraying water behind them with their powerful engines and were shimmering in the distance. I scanned the back of the freighter where I had seen the stowaways. Maybe there was a crack in one corner of one of the containers, I couldn't tell for sure. I scanned the water again. The speedboats were coming so fast. They obviously carried radar, so they would know that we were here also. What would they think of that? What would they think when we disappeared, as we were about to? It was possible they were carrying sonar, but they couldn't search for us with sonar while they were moving so fast and making so much noise. When we disappeared from their radar they would probably just scratch their heads.

I turned the binoculars towards the freighter again. Why did she suddenly seem bigger than before? I climbed inside and looked at the radar. We were only half a mile away! She had been slowing down all the time and I hadn't noticed because I was so busy watching the speedboats. I climbed out and looked at them again. They were completely black, not recreational boaters at all. They were just a couple of minutes away now. The freighter was slowing down and was probably going to stop. Who had the authority to stop a freighter at full sail? Well, the coastguard, of course, or the navy. In fact, the whole situation was starting to have the feel of a military exercise at sea. I remembered stumbling into one on our maiden voyage. It was time to get the heck out of here.

I pulled off the harness. But just as I was about to climb inside and dive, one of the stowaways crawled out of the container again and started trying to climb down towards the deck of the ship. It was a desperate attempt. It would have been difficult for anyone but he was clearly not strong enough to do it. He seemed barely able to stand up. I was pretty sure he was going to fall. Why was he trying so hard to escape? Did they know that the ship was being intercepted and were trying to avoid getting caught? Were they carrying some sort of short-wave radio and were picking up reports that they had been spotted? He wouldn't survive if he jumped. That much I knew. And if he did survive the jump, he could never swim to land. It was too far.

We had to leave *now* and yet . . . I couldn't. What if he jumped before the speedboats arrived? What if he fell? He would die. How could I leave knowing that?

So, I stayed. I cranked up the engine full blast and closed the distance. What if the stowaway jumped while the speedboats were tying up on the port side of the freighter? I couldn't sail away and let him drown. Nor could I stand by and watch. I had to sail closer.

And so I did. It's funny the things that go through your mind at times like this. As I sailed in under the shadow of the gargantuan ship and watched the stowaway cling to one end of a container like a monkey too tired to climb any more, I thought of the people I knew who would do exactly what I was doing right now. I knew without hesitation that Ziegfried would do exactly the same; he would risk getting caught before he would think of saving himself. Sheba would also. It would never cross her mind to think of anyone but the poor stowaway in danger. Then I thought of my grandfather and grandmother, and I felt certain that they, too, for all their old-fashioned ways and criticism of my decisions, would put the life of the stowaway ahead of their own, because that's the sort of people they were. And I felt very grateful to have been raised by such people.

But then I thought of my father and I had to wonder. I wondered if maybe that was what my grandfather had been hinting at when he said he was not like me. Was that it? Was my father the sort of person to put himself first, and was that why he had left when I was born? It seemed a fair question but of course I couldn't answer it now. Maybe in another week I could.

What I was most afraid of happening was exactly what did happen. One of the speedboats came to the port side of the ship; the other swung around to the stern, spotted us and raced over. How I wanted to submerge and disappear. How I wished we could. But every time I thought we might, the stowaway slipped a little and almost fell. It was agonizing watching him. And now, it was too late. The speedboat was upon us. Three officers were on board it. One had crawled out onto the bow with a cable and hook in his hand. Before I could do or explain anything, he jumped onto the hull of the sub, reached down and snapped the hook onto a handle on the side. My heart sank. We had been captured.

Chapter 6

ALL I COULD THINK of was how to escape. And I would if I got the chance. I was pretty sure I could snap that cable if I could just get inside and dive. But the officer standing on the hull was carrying a machine-gun and watching me. He was wearing a grin of satisfaction on his face and shook his head at me. "That cable's a lot stronger than it looks, son. You wouldn't want to be pulling us to the bottom of the river now."

How did he know what I was thinking?

"I wasn't thinking that," I said. "I was just wondering why you're chasing me instead of the stowaways."

The grin dropped off his face and he looked very suspiciously at me. "How did you know we were looking for stowaways?"

I was right. The stowaways had been spotted. He glared at me. He probably figured I had something to do with them. I pointed to the freighter. "They're up there."

He turned and looked up. The man who had crawled out of the container was dangling dangerously by one arm. He was going to fall. And then, he did! He dropped like a bird out of the sky. It was awful.

The officer looked over at his boat quickly, ripped the walkie-talkie from his belt and shouted into it. *"Found them!"*

He pointed to the stern of the freighter. Then he looked back at me. Then he looked back at the freighter, then his boat, waiting for a command. He didn't know what to do.

"Rescue him!" I shouted.

He stared at me wildly, as if he couldn't make up his mind. He shouted into his walkie-talkie again and looked expectantly towards the speedboat.

The officers in the boat shook their heads emphatically. Whatever he was asking, the answer was no. I felt an extreme impatience with him. What was he waiting for? I was ready to jump into the water and swim to the drowning man, but it was nearly two hundred feet still. He would be gone before I could get there.

"He's *drowning*!" I yelled.

Didn't he care? In frustration the officer grabbed hold of the cable and unhooked it from the sub. A wave of relief ran cautiously through me. He jumped back to his boat but turned angrily and yelled at me. "Don't you even *think* of moving!"

I stared back but didn't answer. They churned up the water with the powerful engines on the back of their boat and took off. I watched them rush to the spot where the man had hit the water. They were there in seconds. I hoped it was soon enough. I hoped the stowaway was going to be okay, but didn't see how he could be. It was such a terrible fall.

There wasn't anything I could do to help now. In fact, I was just in the way because I was a distraction to the rescue. No doubt those navy officers wouldn't see it that way but there was no way I was going to hang around until they came back. I needed to get away and hide. I was already an outlaw; leaving wasn't going to make it any worse.

And so I jumped inside, shut the hatch, hit the dive switch and went down to three hundred feet. A quick glance at the charts showed the bottom lying between seven and eight hundred feet. We had lots of room.

Anticosti Island was probably the best place to hide even though it was farther than the shore of Quebec. In the reef surrounding the island the sub could blend in with rocks and underwater formations that would make it nearly impossible to identify. And we could spend time on the beach and wait until they gave up searching for us. And Hollie would be happy with that.

But there was always the chance those speedboats were

carrying sonar and could track us if they wanted to. Tracking a submerged, silently moving submarine from a noisy, racing speedboat was probably impossible. Sonar is far from a perfect science. But if they had other boats in the area and could spread out and set up a sonar net they would have a good chance of finding us. I didn't want to give them that chance. I also didn't want them to know which direction we were heading. And so, I engaged the batteries and motored due east. I sailed about five miles, surfaced and switched on radar. Now they could detect us. I wanted them to. A third boat was on the scene. As soon as we appeared on their radar, one of the three boats came speeding in our direction. I cranked up the engine full blast and made a show of running for the east, as if we were planning to leave the river mouth all together. As they closed to three miles, I switched to battery power again and slipped beneath the waves. Once we were under the surface, I went down to three hundred feet again, shut everything off, turned around, climbed up on the bicycle and pedalled as quietly as a sea turtle towards Anticosti Island.

I pedalled for hours. Hollie lay on his blanket with his head on his paws and watched patiently. He wanted to get out and run. Seaweed looked like he was watching with one eye open but was probably sleeping. I took short breaks, drank orange juice and tried to stay relaxed, but it was hard to when I couldn't know if we were being tracked from above. Probably we weren't. I knew that. But I also couldn't know for certain if we were keeping a true course. Without sonar I couldn't know if we had run into a current that had shifted our direction a few degrees. That was worrisome. But I didn't want to turn on sonar because there was always the chance our sonar waves would bounce off a nearby vessel with a sensitive listening device and they would know exactly where we were. To stay calm and pass the time I opened a book on the handlebars and read about Anticosti Island.

It was bigger than Prince Edward Island but only two hundred people lived there; two hundred people and a hundred thousand deer. Wow! The island used to be privately owned until the Quebec government bought it in 1974. Adolph Hitler tried to buy it in 1937. Holy smokes! Imagine Hitler living in Canada. The Canadian government said no. Good thing. It was bad enough the island was a disaster for ships. Actually, it was a graveyard, just like Sable Island. I bet there were ghosts there.

According to Sheba it was difficult to get close to a ghost. That had certainly been my experience, *if* what I had seen was a ghost. Ziegfried didn't think so. I still wasn't sure.

Ghosts were timid creatures, Sheba said. They were like shadows or wisps of smoke or ripples on the water. She said that ghosts were the spirits of people who hadn't completely left the world because there was something holding them back, something bothering them too much to leave. So, they just sort of flitted about for a while, visiting places and occasionally being seen by people who were sympathetic towards them and didn't scare them. People like her. Well, I supposed that explained why people rarely saw them.

If any place would have ghosts hanging around, surely it was Anticosti Island? Not only had people drowned there when their ships smashed against the rocks, but there was a man, a couple of hundred years ago, who helped people escape their sinking ships, imprisoned them, killed them and ate them! Yikes! How creepy was that?

After three hours of pedalling I surfaced to periscope depth and continued by battery. I couldn't know if we were within radar range of the speedboats and had to assume that we were. I was drop-dead tired now but couldn't risk getting caught again. Besides, I had promised Hollie a walk on the beach. And so, I motored on for a few more hours, until the silhouette of the island appeared under the moon. I sailed in very cautiously with sonar, dropped anchor in thirty feet of water, inflated the dinghy and we climbed in.

According to the charts, the water was crowded with sunken ships, just as at Sable Island. Storms and undertows pushed those wrecks around, too, so that they could appear and disappear randomly, sticking out of the sand and water here and there like skeletons that kept changing their minds about where they wanted to be buried. I didn't want to get the anchor tangled up in the timbers of an old wreck, and I didn't want to strike one of the rocks that had deceived so many other sailors.

I pulled the dinghy onto the beach and Hollie jumped out and ran around like someone who had been locked up for years. He ran so hard he fell over and rolled like a ball. He was crazy. Seaweed was already on the beach, picking long stringy things out of the body of something dead. The sun was still two hours away but there was enough light from the moon to see silhouettes on the beach. The beach was littered with driftwood and rocks and reminded me of pictures I had seen of the surface of the moon, except that the silhouettes seemed to be moving as we walked. I knew they weren't.

We went all the way down the beach, and I had the feeling we were being watched the whole time. We both kept turning around, and Hollie would sniff the air, but he would do that anyway. Eventually he ran the craziness out of his system and started behaving like a normal dog. He turned and looked at me as if he had just woken from a wild dream. What was *that* about?

"I don't know, Hollie. You're the one running around like a nut."

Then we heard a noise and both turned our heads. "What was that?"

He sniffed the air. It had been a strange sound. I couldn't describe it. It wasn't a human sound. There were a hundred thousand deer on this island; maybe it was one of them. I listened closely but heard only the sound of the wind. Maybe what we had heard was a piece of falling driftwood. We reached the end of the beach, turned around and walked back. Hollie trotted beside me like a model dog. If there were any ghosts I thought we might see a bundle of light. But we didn't. If there were any ghosts they were probably afraid of us anyway.

We climbed back into the sub, deflated the dinghy, pulled up anchor and motored a little way from shore. Anxiously, I switched on radar. If there were boats in the area they would know that we were here, or that *somebody* was here. If they came towards us to investigate we'd have to find another place to hide. But I hoped they wouldn't. I was so tired.

The radar wave made a clean sweep across the screen. There was nothing out there. Yes! I started to look for a place to sleep. I took one last peek through the periscope at the beach we had just walked down, now retreating behind us in the dark, and saw a bundle of light! Yikes! Straining my eyes I saw a figure standing at the water's edge, on the very spot we had just stood! It was watching us leave.

"We're going back!" I said excitedly.

Now I was spooked.

Chapter 7

IT DIDN'T SURPRISE me that when I surfaced and opened the hatch the ghost was gone. I still wanted to go and stand on that spot. I planned to leave Hollie in the sub this time but he would have none of that. If I were going to walk on the beach again then so was he. So, I tossed the anchor, inflated the dinghy all over again, climbed in and paddled to the spot. This time, when we stepped onto the beach, Hollie growled. I looked around.

"What is it, Hollie? What do you smell?"

I couldn't see anything, but what was that sound? Was it whispering? Was it the wind? And what was that smell? It smelled like burning leaves or something. Hollie continued to growl but didn't bark. I went and stood where I thought I had seen the figure standing and I felt a shiver go down my spine. The air was cold. I closed my eyes and listened, but all I could hear was the wind and waves, and the little murmur of Hollie's growl, growing fiercer and more afraid at the same time. And then, something coughed behind us.

I turned and saw a towering shape facing us. Its eyes were flashing with the light of the moon. Its head was enormous. It coughed again and snorted. Then I knew what it was. It was a huge buck with an enormous set of antlers. It was standing above us on the beach and pawing the sand with its front hoof. Was it going to charge?

"Bark! Hollie! Bark!"

Hollie barked. The buck snorted again. Then Hollie started barking and didn't stop. It was such a pathetic little bark but the buck backed up and trotted away, snorting like a steam engine.

"Good job, Hollie. You scared him away."

I bent down and patted him. He was trembling. Who would have guessed that a deer would be scarier than a ghost?

We returned to the sub, deflated the dinghy and climbed back in. But when I pulled on the anchor this time, it wouldn't budge. In my haste to see the ghost, I had thrown the anchor too quickly. The current had shifted the sub, the anchor dragged and wrapped around something. Which-ever way I pulled, it would not give. Rats! I would have to swim down and free it. The sun would be up soon. I decided to make a cup of tea and feed the crew first. Seaweed probably wasn't hungry after his breakfast on the beach but he would eat anyway. Seagulls had bottomless stomachs. They were like garbage compactors.

Sitting on the hull drinking my tea and eating an orange, I dangled my feet over the edge and watched as the sun began to pierce the water below. Suddenly, I got a fright. I shouldn't have, really, it was just a wreck beneath us, but it was such a spooky wreck, with open ribs reaching up towards us. The sub looked like a baby dolphin waiting to be grabbed by a giant squid!

I was already kind of jumpy because of the buck. Now, this ship's skeleton looked like it had trapped our anchor on purpose and was trying to grab us. Was it just a coincidence we had stopped directly above it? I knew that Ziegfried would probably just laugh at that, but a chill swept over me and I had to calm myself. Get a grip, I told myself. It was just a coincidence. Like it or not, I had to go down there and free the anchor or we weren't going anywhere.

The problem with letting yourself become afraid of something is that your fear can run away with you. I long ago learned how important it is to face your fears right away and not let them build up until you are too afraid to do anything. There is nothing to be afraid of but fear itself. That's what Ziegfried always said. Fear is explainable, just like everything else.

I finished my orange, took a few deep breaths and jumped off the sub. We were in only thirty feet of water. That was nothing. I could dive to a hundred feet and hold my breath underwater for over two minutes. This dive was nothing, and yet, something about the way the old ship was lying on the bottom spooked me. And it was harder to hold your breath when you were spooked.

Her rib cage looked like a trap ready to snap shut. Each waterlogged rib was tall and curved inward, like a gloomy statue bending over and staring down at you. Swimming down between them I saw the anchor tangled up in the ship's belly, exactly in the middle of the ribs.

It took only fifteen seconds to reach the bottom. The little anchor had wedged itself into a crack in the ship's wooden spine and the rope had twisted up awkwardly on a couple of timbers. I pulled the rope free first, or thought I did, then reached down and tugged at the anchor. It was stuck. Bringing my feet down to balance against the spine, I took hold of the anchor with both hands and prepared to pull harder. Suddenly, something hit me on the back, knocked the air out of my lungs and pinned me down against the spine. It didn't take long to realize what had happened. One of the timbers had collapsed. It hurt my back but I was okay. I didn't panic. That was the important thing. But the timber also fell onto the rope, and the rope was wrapped around my leg. When I tried to free myself from underneath the timber, the rope held me back. I started to feel my lack of air. I pulled hard on my leg, but it wouldn't budge! *That's* when I panicked. I tugged once, tugged twice, then pulled my leg free, but not before the timber cut my skin and filled my knee with splinters. As I swam to the surface I saw that my leg was bleeding.

I broke the surface and gasped for air. My leg was stinging and burning. I climbed onto the sub to take a look. There was a gash about three inches long just above my knee. It wasn't deep. I could clean it and bandage it. But the splinters were a different story. Instead of thin, sharp slivers of wood, they were thick, dull chunks that had become embedded in my skin like rocks. And they hurt! I'd have to pick them out with tweezers and put peroxide on my leg so it wouldn't get infected. But first, I had to swim back down and free the anchor. I had no intention of becoming another wreck on Anticosti Island.

It took a while to calm down. I *hated* panicking, even a little. It was the worst feeling in the world. When you panicked, you lost control of your ability to think. You were just trying to survive. But you didn't make good decisions. It was okay in a situation like that, where all I had to do was pull my leg free. Without panicking maybe I wouldn't have pulled hard enough to free myself and might have drowned. So, maybe it had saved my life. But there were times when I would have drowned if I had panicked, because I really needed to think straight. As Ziegfried always said, the sea doesn't care if you are sincere. If you make a critical mistake, the sea will drown you. It won't take long either.

I breathed deeply and went down again. This time, I kept

an eye on the timbers the whole time, never turning my back on them, and still another one fell! Boy, did I ever get the feeling this old wreck was trying to trap me!

The anchor came free with a good hard tug. Looking up, I saw the timbers reaching for the sub like the limbs of a sea monster and suddenly I remembered Sheba's dream. Was *that* a coincidence? Sheba said there was no such thing as a coincidence. But what else would you call it?

Standing on the hull, I pulled the anchor. The sun was up and the day was clear. Anticosti Island looked different now in the daylight. It was beautiful. It looked like a peaceful giant asleep in a friendly river mouth. How different from the night. It bothered me that I had let myself get spooked. On the other hand, I didn't know why I ever doubted Sheba in the first place; the island was obviously haunted by ghosts. And it was guarded by gigantic deer.

Chapter 8

OKAY. TWO BAD things had happened and we weren't even on the river yet. Was something trying to tell me to turn around and go back home? Sheba said that something terrible would happen but that I would be all right. Well, I guessed it had happened. *Two* terrible things had happened. This voyage was a lot more trouble than I thought it would be. Was it worth it?

It was my fault though, I had to admit. We had been caught by the navy because I sailed too closely behind the freighter. I got trapped by the wreck because I had thrown the anchor carelessly in my hurry to see the ghost. If I had done just what I was supposed to do—sail to Montreal—

instead of looking at other things and procrastinating, probably nothing bad would have happened. Probably. On the other hand, I was an explorer by nature. I had to explore things. I couldn't help it.

I was so desperately tired and needed to sleep, but had to clean my wounds first. The waterlogged wood was like mud. The splinters didn't come out in neat pieces so I had to scrape them out, which hurt a lot and made them bleed. Then, the peroxide hurt even more. I spent two hours cleaning the wounds, feeling sleepier all the time. When I finished, I laid my head down on my cot for just a second. We were still on the surface and the hatch was wide open. I only intended to rest for a second.

It was twilight when I woke. Hollie was sitting beneath the open portal chewing on a rope. He wagged his tail and came over when I lifted my head. I reached down and scratched his fur. He was the best dog in the world. I had always wanted a dog growing up and never had one. I found Hollie in a drifting dory one day. Someone had put a rope around his neck, tied it to a stone and thrown him off a wharf in the fog. How horrible can people be? But he landed in a dory, it drifted free, or someone *set* it free, and I found him. Nobody had wanted him. Nobody had cared about him. He was an orphan.

"But you're a sailor now, aren't you?"

His little tail beat against the floor.

"Where's Seaweed?"

He looked up the portal towards the sky, growing dark now.

"Yup. Probably eating something on the beach. Time to go. He'll find us."

I started the engine and turned west, into the current. My leg was swollen around the area where I had scraped the splinters out and it was sore. I wrapped a bandage around it and opened it every few hours to pour peroxide on it, the way my grandmother had taught me. That was really painful. But better a painful leg than to have drowned.

Jacques Cartier never had trouble on Anticosti Island, according to Sheba's book. He never lost a single member of his crew either, at least not at sea. That was kind of hard to believe when you think that shipwrecks were common then and a sailor's life so dangerous. If airplane crashes today were as common as shipwrecks back then, no one would ever fly.

Sailors died of accidents on board the ships too, and disease, and yet Cartier never lost a single crew member in all of his voyages. He must have been pretty smart. He must have been very determined too. Hmmm. I decided to stop whining. It was true: I never wanted to go to Montreal in the first place, but I had *agreed* to go. And so, I figured I'd better smarten up and try a little harder to make this trip successful. Either go, or don't go, I thought to myself, but don't keep belly-aching about it.

That's what I was thinking when it started to rain.

At first, the rain fell gently. The air was warm and the rain was light. Hollie and I stood in the portal in the dark. I stood on the ladder and leaned against the open hatch. Hollie rested against my chest and arms, his front paws on the hatch. Seaweed finally joined us and sat on the bow in front of us as the sub plowed through the water, splaying waves perfectly even on both sides. It was a windless night and the rain came down straight and sprinkled Hollie's face and made him blink. But soon it started to rain harder, and since we wanted to stay in the portal, I went in and grabbed an umbrella. Usually it was too windy for an umbrella but tonight it was still and it was nice to stand in the portal and listen to the rain falling and smell the river and smell the mustiness of Hollie's fur. Hollie smelled like an old wool blanket when he was wet.

And then it started to rain harder.

The rain came straight down and it poured! Seaweed hopped onto the hatch, squeezed behind us, then dropped inside. The rain beat down so hard on the umbrella it made me laugh. Hollie looked worried but I assured him it was okay.

"We're in a submarine, Hollie. This is the safest place in the world."

I thought maybe after fifteen minutes or so the rain would lighten up but it didn't. Half an hour later it was still flooding down. The air was so wet it was almost hard to breathe. We could have climbed inside but it was so interesting. Sheets of water fell off the umbrella and some of it splashed inside the sub but I didn't care. It would just collect into the drain and the sump pumps would remove it. The submarine really was designed for water, inside and out.

And then I thought I heard the radar beep.

I wasn't sure at first; the rain was so loud. But the beep of the radar had a piercing tone that travelled through the sound of rushing water. I shut the hatch and we went inside. It wasn't a strong signal. It was there one moment, gone the next, then back again. That happens sometimes when an object is riding a wave, submerges then comes back up. It could have been a metal barrel or a container. But there were no waves tonight. The signal was only five miles away and didn't appear to be moving. I wondered why I hadn't heard the radar until now. Since it wasn't far out of our way I decided to investigate.

I had never seen such rain. It never let up, not for a minute. Half a mile from the signal I couldn't see any evidence of a light. Still none at quarter of a mile. Whatever it was, it wasn't very big or well lit. As we closed in on it, I slowed to ten knots, then five, then cut the engine and climbed the portal with the umbrella and tried to see through the rain as we drifted closer. There was something there; I just needed to get a little closer . . . a little closer . . . Oh! We hit something! I heard someone yelling. Then I heard two people yelling. They were speaking French. I turned on our floodlights and scanned the water. I saw a long sea kayak. There was a man and woman in it. She looked frightened and he looked angry. We had struck the kayak but weren't going very fast and I was pretty sure it just bounced off the hull. I couldn't understand what they were yelling because it was in French, so, I pulled on the harness, climbed out and went halfway down the railing.

"Are you all right?" I yelled.

"*Non!*"

"What are you doing out here?"

They were dressed well enough for the weather but carrying only a flimsy light. They must have had some metal somewhere that was showing up unevenly on radar.

"*Nous sommes perdus!*" cried the girl. "We're lost!"

"We're *not* lost!" yelled the guy. "We are just caught in the rain."

"We've been lost all day!" cried the girl. "We're exhausted!"

"*Nous ne sommes pas perdus!*" said the guy. "I know where we are."

"Do you want to come inside and dry out?"

"*C'est un sous-marin?*"

"What?"

"Is that a submarine?"

"Yes."

"Oh! Is it safe?"

I felt like saying it was a heck of a lot safer than where they were right now. "Yes, it's safe, but it'll be a little crowded. Come in slowly and don't scare my seagull, okay? You'll have to sit on the floor."

"*D'accord*. But we must first cover our kayak so it doesn't fill with water. Can we tie it to your submarine?"

"Okay."

I grabbed some rope, tied one end to a handle on the portal and tossed the other to the guy. The girl climbed up first. As she passed me she said, "*Merci beaucoup!* I am Marie. He is Jacques. We were lost all day. I was really afraid."

"You're welcome. I'm Alfred. Please don't touch any switches inside, okay?"

"Okay."

When Jacques climbed up, he said, "We are not lost. It is just rain. It is going to stop any moment."

"I understand. Please don't touch any switches inside, okay?"

"*Oui, oui*. Thank you for stopping for us, hey?"

"You're welcome."

I followed him in and shut the hatch. Seaweed was already on my cot. He wasn't fussy about company, unless they were other seagulls, and would have left had it not been raining so hard.

"Just leave him alone and he'll be okay," I said.

Marie sat beside Hollie and scratched his ears. She was very gentle and Hollie liked her right away. He was a suck for affection.

"What a sweet little doggie!"

"Please sit here," I said to Jacques, and pointed to a spot behind the bicycle seat. "We need to distribute our weight evenly."

"*Oui.* Oh, man, it is amazing in here! Is this where you live?"

"Pretty much. I spend a lot of time at sea."

"You know, I think I have heard of you. You rescued a family a couple of years ago, yes?"

"Yes, I guess so."

"They call you the '*outlaw du sous-marin.*' The 'outlaw of the submarine,' *oui?*"

"I guess so. Something like that."

"But . . . how come they still chase you? Did you steal something? Do you carry guns?"

"No. It's just that my submarine is not registered. To have it registered they would have to inspect it. It probably wouldn't pass their inspection and I probably wouldn't get it back."

"*Ah, tu as bien raison.* My uncle works for the government. He says the government is run by insurance companies now. It is the insurance companies that would shut you down. The government cannot allow you to ride around in an uninsured vessel."

He looked around. "I don't think they would insure you for this."

"I don't think so either."

"So, you become an outlaw. Maybe it is not so bad, hey?"

"It's okay."

"But . . . can they not catch you if they want to?"

"I don't know. Maybe they don't want to."

"They don't want to?"

"It's because he's *helping* people, Jacques," said Marie.

She sounded fed up with him. After a day lost at sea I'd be fed up too.

"How did you get . . . I mean, how is it you got caught in the rain?"

"He still doesn't believe we are lost. It is because he never believes it is dangerous," said Marie, without looking up. "He thinks the water is just as safe as the land. *C'est incroyable!*"

"*Ah! Marie! Tu exagères toujours!* The water is not so dangerous. You just need to know what you are doing."

"Yah! And you know what you are doing! That is why we were lost all day!"

"We were never lost."

"*Dis-lui!* Tell him! Please! Tell him how dangerous the water is."

I didn't want to get caught in the middle of this but I couldn't deny that she was right.

"The sea is very dangerous. And so is the mouth of the river."

"You see? There! You have heard it now from the 'outlaw of the submarine' himself. Please tell him why it is so dangerous."

"Well . . . it is so unpredictable. Weather conditions will change without warning. Storms will blow in your path when you are least expecting them. Then, a miscalculation of your position could be fatal. Last year I came upon a drowned fisherman after a storm. It was really sad."

"*Tu vois, Jacques?* A miscalculation."

Jacques seemed less confident now but didn't want to show it. "I never miscalculated! I know exactly where we are! Once this rain stops, we can continue to Anticosti Island. It is just five kilometres away!"

Boy was he off! But I hated to correct him. I would have hated being corrected in front of my girlfriend, if I ever had a girlfriend. But the truth was it was dangerous for both of them. I was surprised he didn't realize that. I had to find a way to explain it to him without embarrassing him. "Umm . . . I can show you on a chart exactly where our position is now, if you would like."

He looked surprised. "*Oui!* Of course."

"We are . . . here!" I touched the chart with my finger. "And Anticosti Island is . . . here!"

"And that is . . . how many kilometres?"

"Umm . . . it's about twenty miles. Thirty-two kilometres."

"*Oh . . . mon . . . Dieu!*" said Marie.

Jacques stared at the chart, disbelieving. "Are you sure we are here, so far to the west?"

"Absolutely sure. I think probably what happened is that you drifted with the current without knowing it."

"Ahhhh . . ."

He continued to study the chart, but his face grew pale and I could tell he was fighting feelings of embarrassment.

He stole quick glances at Marie but avoided her direct stare. If they had continued the way they had been going, they would have missed Anticosti Island completely and would have been lost at sea. I wondered if he realized that. I wondered if I should tell him. I decided not to.

In less than half an hour Marie was asleep. That didn't surprise me. Being at sea has a way of sucking the energy out of you, especially in bad weather. But Jacques was fidgeting in his sleeping bag. Was his conscience bothering him? Or his pride? A few times I had the sense he was going to get up. It was three hours before sunrise. I set a course for Anticosti Island once more, but headed farther north, correcting for Jacques' loss of position and heading closer to the river at the same time.

An hour before sunrise we were just a few miles offshore. We would have been able to see the island if there had been lights. But there weren't any. Suddenly, Jacques stood up and said that he had to pee. He climbed the portal. I noticed that he took his pack with him. That seemed odd but I didn't say anything. Five minutes later I poked my head through the hatch. He was gone. He vanished like a ghost. The kayak was gone too.

Chapter 9

❧

"NAVAL OFFICERS DISCOVERED *three illegal persons on board a cargo ship in the mouth of the St. Lawrence River yesterday,*" said the radio announcer. "*Officials haven't confirmed the nationality of the stowaways but believe they may be from Somalia. The stowaways were discovered when they exited the container in which they were hiding in search of food and water. One of the stowaways was described as being in critical condition. One unidentified official said the stowaways could have been locked up in their self-imposed confinement for as long as two months.*"

They didn't mention that anyone had died. That was good. He must have survived the fall after all. But man, how those stowaways must have suffered. And now, after all that trouble, they had been caught anyway. I felt sorry for them. The next bit on the radio was interesting too.

"*Reports of an unidentified submarine spotted in the area have not been confirmed. Officials refused to comment. The submarine is not believed to be linked to the stowaways.*"

I wondered if they would have confirmed those reports had they captured me.

The radio had woken Marie. She was devastated when I told her that Jacques had abandoned her. And yet, she didn't seem all that surprised. I wondered if he had done something like that before. He struck me as the sort of person who acted before he thought things through; all enthusiasm and no caution—a dangerous combination at sea.

I made her a cup of tea and carried it over. She had spread out her mat and sleeping bag and looked very cozy with Hollie on her lap. He looked like a baby kangaroo in a pouch. Hollie became attached to people very quickly because he was a dog, but also because he was an orphan. He never seemed to feel that he belonged anywhere except in the sub, and was never happy left alone. I rarely left him alone.

Marie looked so sad. I felt bad for her.

"Did he steal your kayak?"

"No. It was his kayak." She took a deep breath. "I am glad he is gone."

"Really?"

I couldn't tell if she meant that or not. "How long have you known him?"

She wiped a tear. "Seven years."

"Oh."

That was a long time. She scratched Hollie's ears and sighed, then raised her head and looked at me. She was upset but was trying not to show it. Her voice was breaking. "What kind of person leaves you in the middle of the night?"

"I don't know."

"What kind of person leaves you in the middle of the river?"

Actually it was more like the sea. "I don't know."

I knew she wasn't expecting me to answer. I was wondering what kind of person would throw a dog off a wharf. And what kind of person would walk away from his own child? I didn't want to think about those things but couldn't help it. Before Sheba's dream, I didn't think about such things much. Now, I couldn't stop. I didn't like it.

"He is such a child," she said. "He cannot take responsibility for anything, for making us lost, so he runs away like a little boy. *Un enfant immature!*"

I didn't know what to say. I had never seen anyone behave the way Jacques had. Could there be anything worse than abandoning someone in distress? That was beyond me. Wherever he was now, Jacques must have been carrying a heavy conscience. He must have known what he did was wrong?

I couldn't help wonder about my father too, as much as I didn't want to.

Marie was a naturalist. She studied birds and whales and took pictures of them and sold them to magazines. She said it was her dream to share the beauty of the natural world with people. That sounded like a pretty nice dream to me. She said that Jacques was also a naturalist but that he was a lot more interested in experiencing the world than in sharing it. That didn't surprise me.

She said she was from a little village on the Gaspé Peninsula but lived in Quebec City now.

"My grandpapa has a beautiful old farm. It overlooks the river from high up. You would really like it. You could drop me off there, Alfred. It would be nice if you came and visited my grandpapa with me. He would like you. When he was a young man he saw submarines in the river."

"Really?"

"Yes. He and his friends saw German sailors climb out onto the islands and drink and sing and laugh."

"But . . . weren't the sailors afraid of getting caught?"

"I don't know. You have to ask my grandpapa. But he would be happy to tell you. He loves to talk about the war."

"I would love to hear about it. I really would."

I decided to drop Marie off on the riverbank below her grandfather's farm, hide the sub and join her for a short visit. She said I would receive some good old-fashioned

Québécois hospitality. That sounded pretty good.

We sailed on the surface in broad daylight with the hatch wide open. Only a few times did I have to submerge when ships came down the river. Marie didn't mind that too much but preferred when we were on the surface and the hatch was wide open. She said that she didn't like small spaces but that the sub was cozy. She was good company. She taught me lots of things about birds and whales in the river. The St. Lawrence is a kind of portal between saltwater and freshwater worlds, she said. In its mouth are all the saltwater birds, just as out at sea. And there are whales and seals and dolphins. Upriver, the birds are freshwater birds and the fish are freshwater fish, but the whales and seals can only swim partway, to where the salt water and fresh water join together. The water forms a brackish mix there, especially around the mouth of the Saguenay River, which empties into the St. Lawrence. Where the two rivers meet is a hot spot for feeding and spawning and is a favourite spot for beluga whales, the smallest of the whales.

"They're the sweetest ones," said Marie with delight. "But they have been hunted almost to extinction. Scientists hope they will make a comeback now. Belugas are like little children, really. They love to play. They're so friendly. That's why they're so easy to catch, and why so few of them are left."

As we sailed up the mouth of the river, Marie insisted upon sitting on the hull, down in front of the portal—Seaweed's spot, though I didn't think he minded. He spent most of the day soaring above us, when he wasn't sleeping on the stern. I tied a rope around Marie's waist and tied it to the hatch so that she could hold on while she dangled her feet over the side. She said she never realized a submarine could be so much fun.

"I feel like I'm riding a whale! This is the best way to travel in the world!"

Well, I had to agree with that.

Darkness fell as we sailed under the shadow of the Gaspé Peninsula. There was a cliff and rocky hillside. Marie couldn't recognize her grandfather's farm from the water, so I searched for a small cove in which to moor the sub and hide it. I tied it securely with three ropes. There wasn't much current yet, but there was some, and it was flowing consistently in one direction. That was different from having to consider only the tide. Now there was the tide *and* river current. I could not turn my back on the sub unless it was securely moored or anchored.

There was no beach, just a rocky landing below the cliff. Hollie jumped out of the dinghy, stared impatiently at the rocks that were too big for him to jump over, and whined. So I picked him up and we climbed the hill and found a small road where he could run, and then he was happy. We walked to the nearest house. Marie asked to use the phone and called her grandpapa to come and pick us up. In less than an hour, Hollie and I were in the back of an old pickup truck, riding along the road high above the river. Marie and her grandpapa were sitting in the front, talking in French a mile a minute.

Chapter 10

OLD FARMERS AND fishermen have something in common: enormous hands. Like my grandfather, Marie's grandpapa had hands that could crush a coconut. It was as if the strength of their backs and legs went into their hands when they got older. When he shook hands with me it felt like my hand had been caught in a wooden trap. I couldn't move it until he let it go; and he didn't let it go until he had shaken it up and down about ten times. I didn't believe in all my lifetime I would ever have strength like that.

Marie was right; he loved to talk about the war. And he spoke English too. But he didn't hear very well, so we had to shout. Marie and I sat on the floor with a plate of crepes and cups of hot chocolate, like two kids listening to a bedtime story. The crepes were just skinny pancakes filled with fresh strawberries, cream and maple syrup, and they were absolutely delicious. Hollie sat on Marie's lap, sniffed at her crepes and waited for her to pat him, which she did a lot.

Her grandpapa was gentle, but his eyes were wild. Marie said that one of them was made of glass. I didn't want to stare, but one of the eyes kept staring at me. The other one was smaller and wandered around a lot. I couldn't tell which one was the real one.

He hadn't served in the war, he said, because of an accident when he was a boy. That's when he lost his eye. He never told us what the accident was. He said that he and his friends played on the river a lot and that the river was a dangerous place to play. I believed him. As a young man, he floated logs downriver to the sawmill and sometimes rowed his girlfriend out at night to see the lights of the peninsula from the water. It was on one of those nights, in the summer of 1942, that he saw a German U-boat surface in the river.

"She broke the surface like a demon from the deep," he said, with his big eye fixed on me and the smaller one wandering around the room. You could tell that he enjoyed telling the story. "She climbed out of that dark water and pulled herself up on top of the surface and snorted like a beast. She snorted just like a bull! And there she was, not more than a hundred and fifty feet away from us."

"How big was she?"

"Hey?"

"How big was the submarine?"

"Long! Long as a giant eel! Two hundred and fifty feet long! They caught her off the coast of Nova Scotia the next year and sank her. But she sent a dozen ships to the grave first, including the ferry between Port aux Basques and North Sydney. Killed a hundred and thirty-six people that night, before they rammed her."

"They rammed her?"

"Hey?"

"They *rammed* her?"

"Oh, yah! Ran over her like a snake on the road, sent her to the bottom. HMS *Viscount*."

Wow. I tried to picture a ship ramming a submarine. It was like sea monsters fighting. "And the night you saw the submarine?"

"Hey?"

"Tell us about the night you saw the submarine, Grand-papa."

"Oh, yah! She sank the *Carolus* that very night. A big Finnish freighter. Canadian government seized her for the war then the Germans sank her a few days later. Right off Metis Beach."

He jumped to his feet, went to the bookshelf and pulled down a heavy book. As he dropped it onto the table, the book opened by itself to a page where it was creased. He stuck it with his finger. Then, he pointed out the window towards the river. "She's out there!"

I leaned closer and saw an old black and white photo of a merchant steamer with a single smokestack in her centre. She was over three hundred feet long! Now, she lay on the river bottom. I wondered if we would see her on our way.

"Were you afraid?"

"Hey?"

"Were you *afraid*, Grandpapa?"

He laughed. "Oh, yah! I was afraid. But they were nice enough."

"What? They saw you?"

"Hey?"

"Did they *see you*, Grandpapa?"

"Yah! They saw me and they waved to me. They were just regular sailors like anybody else. Caught up in the war. They sank the *Carolus*, and then it was their turn. War doesn't play favourites."

War doesn't play favourites. His words stayed in my mind after we left. They reminded me of Ziegfried's saying: the sea doesn't care if you are sincere. Beware all who sail. True enough. Some of us cannot resist it still.

Marie stayed the night. Hollie and I returned to the sub. He hated to leave. I knew he would. His only consolation was that it meant another walk. Marie's grandpapa was horrified that we would leave so late at night, but she told him I wanted to sleep on my boat. She never told him it was a submarine.

We planned to meet in the afternoon the next day. She

would sail with us as far as Quebec City. We didn't usually take passengers but she was used to the sub now and we were going there anyway. It seemed like a good idea at the time.

When Hollie and I returned to the sub, I was shocked at what we found. We had moored at high tide. Now, the tide was out. The sub was sitting on the river bottom! It was exposed! Thank heavens it was dark. I would have to wait an hour or so for the tide to reverse enough before we were even able to move! I knew the tide came up the river but never dreamed it would change the river's height *that* much. I wouldn't make that mistake again.

I paddled the dinghy over and we climbed in. I hated the feeling of the sub not moving, and was only happy when the river returned enough to lift us free. I motored to a deeper spot, tied up again to rocks but left enough slack in the ropes to allow for the tide. Then I submerged to periscope depth and went to bed. Seaweed was still out but he would have no trouble spotting us. Chances were he'd be sitting on the periscope when I woke.

It was late afternoon when I peeked through the periscope and saw Marie sitting patiently on a rock. The tide had come and gone once more and we were able to motor closer to shore again. I surfaced awash, showing the portal merely a foot above the surface, and kept the hull hidden. I inflated the dinghy, rowed over and picked her up. She was carrying her pack and holding a bag with a dozen crepes and a Thermos of hot chocolate. Her face was beaming. If she were sad about Jacques, she was dealing with it well.

"How exciting is this?" she said. "We're sailing to Quebec City in a submarine! Will you let me look out of the periscope, Alfred?"

"Sure."

"Oh! Wonderful!"

Marie's grandpapa had said that the *Carolus* was lying just outside in the river but the map suggested she had actually sunk a hundred miles upstream. No one had found her yet. We went up against the retreating tide, which I measured at almost four knots with the current, although the current seemed to change easily depending upon depth and other things such as the wind. It was tricky. Marie stood at the periscope and kept an eye on other vessels while I watched the screens, studied the map and tried to determine our true speed.

"I see a ship! Oh! I see another one! This is so exciting! They are passing so close to us and they don't even know we are here!"

We were sailing under battery power, submerged, at thirteen knots. Our true speed against the land was probably only about nine knots. As soon as the tide reversed, the current reversed and the river actually flowed backwards! Then, our true speed was closer to sixteen knots, but I was mostly just guessing because it was too hard to determine speed accurately when it was constantly changing. It took us all evening and most of the night to reach Metis Beach. At least we were able to ride on the surface after dark and sail by engine. We arrived in the middle of the night, dropped anchor in thirty feet of water in high tide and went to sleep for just a couple of hours. We set the alarm for a few minutes before sunrise. I didn't want anyone spotting us when the sun came up. We wanted to look for the wreck in daylight as we passed. I dropped onto my bunk and fell asleep instantly. Hollie curled up with Marie on her sleeping bag and I heard her whisper sweetly to him as I drifted off.

Chapter 11

WE NEVER HAD a chance of finding the *Carolus*. I should have realized that. The river was too murky and way too deep. A few miles offshore the bottom fell to a thousand feet! It was fifty miles between banks still. That was some river! Maybe, if we made hundreds of passes back and forth, crisscrossing like a spider's web, we might have picked her up on sonar. Maybe. But we could never go down there, not even close, and could never even peek at her. I had other things I was supposed to be doing anyway, like getting to Montreal and back.

So, we moved on. An hour and a half later, we found another wreck. It was lying in our path in only a hundred and thirty feet of water and it was gigantic!

The *Empress of Ireland* was the biggest naval disaster in Canadian history, not counting the Halifax Explosion, and I had never even heard of it. Marie told me all about it but I could hardly believe it. In 1914, the giant luxury ocean-liner, five hundred and seventy feet long, was sailing down the river from Quebec City when she collided with another ship, tore up her bow and sank like a stone. Within minutes, over a thousand people drowned. This was kind of hard for me to grasp. The *Empress of Ireland* was as long as eleven of Cartier's ships in a row! That was unbelievable! Now, she was lying in only a hundred and thirty feet of water. If she stood on end, four hundred and forty feet of her would stick out of the water. Talk about a sea monster! And yet, as we slowed to a drift above the wreck, just offshore from Rimouski, the river was peaceful and friendly. You would never know such a monstrous vessel lay beneath the river's gentle flow, or that such a terrible tragedy had taken place here, one of the greatest tragedies Canada has ever known.

But there was more.

Marie said that the *Empress* was carrying a sarcophagus with a princess from ancient Egypt. A mummy. And the mummy was supposedly cursed and believed to have caused the disaster.

"Whoa! That's crazy," I said. "Do you believe that?"

"Not really. But a lot of people did. And some say that the wreck is cursed still."

"Why?"

"Because a lot of divers have died here, looking for treasure and stuff. And bodies and parts of bodies have washed out of the wreck ever since it went down."

"Creepy. Do you believe in ghosts?"

"No. Do you?"

"I'm not sure."

Marie ran her fingers through Hollie's fur. "I believe in the Loch Ness monster."

"What? You don't believe in ghosts but you believe in the Loch Ness *monster*?"

"Yes."

"Why?"

"Because ghosts are not from this world, but large creatures have always existed, especially in the deep. In prehistoric times they were *really* big. And, we have other prehistoric creatures around today, like the coelacanth."

She put her face to Hollie's face. "You're precious."

"The what?"

"The coelacanth. A fish from the dinosaur age. We used to only find fossils of them. Then, fishermen started catching them in their nets."

"Cool."

"So . . . that's why I believe there is a huge creature deep in Loch Ness."

We were gliding through the water on battery power at periscope depth. Visibility was about ten feet through the observation window, but a murky visibility, nothing like at sea. A hundred feet down, visibility would be even worse. No doubt that contributed to the danger of diving at such a wreck. A bigger danger, I imagined, was the size of her. Divers would swim inside, become lost and their air would run out. That's what happened to underwater cave divers sometimes. Diving was a dangerous hobby.

It didn't take long to find the *Empress* with sonar. She was enormous! We were like a little bug in the water above her. Marie sat close to the window, leaning on her elbows and staring down. Hollie stared too but was just pretending. He never took an interest in the observation window because he couldn't smell anything through it. It was just part of the decoration of his living space.

We descended slowly but I warned Marie that the wreck might appear very suddenly and scare her.

"*Oh, mon Dieu!* This is probably the most exciting thing I've ever done!"

I was glad. You got used to seeing wrecks when you lived in a submarine. All the same, I was a little excited too.

"I'll turn on the floodlights when we're closer. We won't see much without those. And we'll never be able to see the whole ship, just parts of it as we pass over it."

Down, down, down we drifted, quite slowly because even with sonar it was difficult to tell if there were pieces of the ship sticking up, and I didn't want to hit anything.

"Sixty feet."

"I don't see anything."

"You won't see anything yet."

"It's pretty dark."

"I'll hit the lights at seventy-five feet."

"This is kind of spooky."

"Be warned. It might scare you."

"It can't be that scary. It's just old twisted metal under water, right?"

"Yes, but . . . it can look pretty scary. Seventy feet . . . seventy-five . . . here are the lights."

"Wow. They're really bright. But I still don't see anything."

"You will. Eighty feet."

"Nothing."

"Eighty-five feet."

"Nothing."

I smiled. It was fun having Marie on board.

"Ninety feet."

"Noth—ahhhhhh!"

Marie screamed and jumped away from the window. Hollie ran over to me and hid between my feet. I picked him up, stopped the sub and came to the window. Marie's eyes were wide with fear but she was quickly calming down.

"*Oh . . . mon . . . Dieu!* That scared the heck out of me! It's just so . . . spooky! Look at it!"

I scratched Hollie's ears and looked down through the window.

"Yup. There she is."

Marie took a deep breath.

"Sorry for screaming. It just caught me off guard. It looks like it is reaching up at us, trying to grab us."

The sub's bright lights created a world of shadows, and the river current created movement, so there were lots of things to look at besides old twisted metal. Long, stringy weeds stuck out of holes everywhere and waved like tentacles. The current pulled patches of debris in and out of dents and holes and they really did look sometimes like they were reaching up at us. But Marie calmed down.

"Wow! It's like looking at another planet. I mean, I've seen such things on TV, of course, but somehow, when it's right outside your window, it's different."

The wreck was pretty beaten up, as wrecks always are. There were gashes in her side and huge holes that we could even have sailed through. But I would never take such a risk. My experience with the old wooden wreck at Anticosti Island was still fresh in my mind. My leg was still sore.

We glided over the entire wreck, much of which was covered by silt. No doubt the river would eventually hide all traces of her, just as sand from the Sahara Desert blew into the Mediterranean Sea and covered ancient temples and cities the sea had swallowed. I learned that on our second voyage. Given enough time, the powers of nature can hide anything.

We turned, dropped a little closer and glided over the wreck again. It was so interesting. Two hours passed like nothing. I was feeling a little concerned for Seaweed because I knew he couldn't spot us. And then, Marie saw something.

"Alfred?"

"Yes?"

"What's *that*?"

I came over and looked down. "I don't know."

"But what do you think it is?"

"I don't know, but I suppose it looks like a person bent in half."

"It does, doesn't it? Do you think it's a body?"

I looked harder. "It probably isn't. Things have a way of looking like something else underwater, especially when they've been there for a long time. Chances are, if you touched it, it would be nothing but a big clump of weeds stuck together."

"Do you think we should try to get closer just in case it's a body? Because, if it is a body, then we have to report it."

"Hmmm."

I didn't really want to move closer because there were so many tentacles dangling free, and while most were surely just weeds, some of them could be old rope, or even metal cables. I didn't want to get the propeller wrapped up in a cable.

"Just a little closer. Then we can see what it is."

"Okay. Just a little closer."

But it wasn't easy to move just a little closer. The current across the surface of the wreck was creating a turbulence that I didn't realize until we were almost touching it. Before I knew what was happening the sub started to tilt sideways.

"What's happening?"

"Umm . . . just a bit of turbulence, but we'd better get out of here."

And then I heard the motor whine. "Shoot!" I raced to the panel and shut the power off.

"What? What happened?"

I ignored Marie's question. I was too preoccupied. I stared down through the observation window and watched to see if we would drift free. We didn't. Slowly the sub turned and faced away from the current, like a kite on a string.

"What is it, Alfred? What happened?"

"Ummm . . . there's a cable jammed in the propeller."

"Oh! No!"

"No, it's okay. Don't worry. Everything's fine. It's no big deal."

"Oh. That's good. I was frightened there for a moment."

I didn't want to lie to Marie—this had never happened before—but I couldn't let her panic. I needed to sit calmly and think it through and make smart choices. To do that, I needed her to be calm. The truth was: we were stuck.

Chapter 12

MY MIND RACED through the possibilities and I had to keep slowing it down. It was so important to think clearly. When a cable was wrapped around the propeller, the thing to do was go out and unwrap it by hand. If we were on the surface, that's exactly what I would have done. But we were a hundred feet down. Since that was my maximum depth for diving it was not impossible for me to go out, unwrap the cable, swim to the surface, catch my breath and swim back down. But, of course, I couldn't get out without flooding the sub. When we built the sub, we tested it for exactly that—flooding. We sank it twice on purpose, and I practised opening and sealing the hatch underwater, and sealing myself inside when the sub was filled with water, which was certainly one of the scariest feelings in the world. The hatch now had an automatic sealing mechanism. The sub would flood, but the hatch would shut by itself and the sump pumps would remove the water, but not as fast as it would rush in. We had tested for that too. Ziegfried had insisted upon testing everything. I understood his obsession for testing better all the time.

The sump pumps could not keep up with water flooding through an open portal. The hatch would have to open and shut immediately. If it didn't for any reason, the sub would fill completely in just seconds. And though I would probably survive by swimming to the surface, Hollie and Marie wouldn't.

"What are you thinking, Alfred?"

"What? Oh. I'm just thinking it through. Don't worry. It'll be fine."

"That's good. I was so worried. What will you do?"

"Well, there are a number of ways to fix the problem. I just have to decide which method I want to try first."

"But what if it doesn't work?"

I stared at Marie and tried to look as calm as possible, even bored. "It's no big deal. It'll just hold us up for a little while. I just don't want to damage my propeller. Give me a few minutes to figure out the best way to unhook the cable, okay?"

She nodded her head and went back to combing Hollie's

fur with her fingers. I suddenly regretted having a passenger. It hadn't struck me before just how much responsibility it was. It was a lot! This was my vessel and I was the captain. Marie's safety, her life actually, was completely in my hands. I didn't like that feeling. I didn't feel old enough for that kind of responsibility yet.

Most likely what happened was that a cable had been pulled into the whirl of the propeller and twisted around it, stopping its spin. That's why the motor started whining; the driveshaft was blocked. The motor was not designed to push against dead resistance. That was almost certainly what had happened, though I couldn't know for certain without looking. Since the cable likely twisted up in one direction, it was possible that it would release if I put the motor in reverse. That might work. The only thing I didn't like about that was that every time the propeller pushed against the dead resistance of the cable, it risked getting damaged or even snapping off. Then, we'd have no propulsion at all. The sub would surface, but it would free-float down the river. Oh boy, what a disaster that would be!

I had an idea. Instead of engaging the batteries to turn the driveshaft, I could simply pedal the bike. If I spun the pedal very slowly, I could turn the propeller just a little. I climbed onto the bike and tried pedalling in reverse. Nope. Nothing. Then I tried forward. Nope. The propeller wouldn't budge. Shoot!

"Is it working?" said Marie.

I could tell she was trying hard to stay calm.

"Ummm . . . just a minute."

Man, I wished she wasn't here! I realized it wouldn't bother me as much if Hollie and I drowned as much as if she did, strange as that was to think. We were sailors. It was a risk we lived with every day and it was a choice we had made. Even though Hollie was just a dog, I knew he felt the same way, I just knew it. Marie was our passenger. She was our responsibility. Gosh, I wished she wasn't here now.

I tried raising the sub just a little. I pumped air into the tanks and we rose about five feet. The cable didn't let go. I pumped air out of the tanks and we fell and bumped the wreck, and that made a loud noise.

"Oh! What was that?"

"Nothing. We just bumped the wreck a little. No big deal."

Without being able to turn the propeller I couldn't even turn the sub around to look at the cable. It was so frustrating!

"Is there anyone we can call?" said Marie. She sounded alarmed.

"Yes. I can float a cable to the surface and call for help if we need to. But I don't want to do that just yet, okay? Please don't worry. I'll get us out of here."

"But you will call if you have to, right? Promise?"

"Yes, I promise. I will call for sure if we need to."

"I think it's cursed, Alfred."

"*What?*"

"The wreck. I think it's cursed, just like they say. Really, I do."

Marie was shivering with fear now. That was understandable. I just hoped she wouldn't panic. I wouldn't know how to deal with her panic.

"I don't think it's cursed, Marie. We just got stuck on a cable. It was our own fault. We went too close to the wreck."

"But so many people died here! This place is a graveyard . . ."

She was biting her lip, holding onto Hollie and starting to cry. At least she was trying not to panic. I had to figure out something fast. If I did call for help, it would take hours before anyone could come. They'd have to put boats in the water and send divers down. All they'd have to do is release the cable. But they would surely seize the sub. And everything would be photographed and filmed for the news. My exploring days would be over.

"Will you call, Alfred?"

"Yes . . . just give me a chance . . ."

If it were just Hollie and me, I could open the hatch and go out. I felt confident I could open and shut the hatch. The sub would fill half, maybe even three quarters, with water, and Hollie would have to swim, but the sump pumps would keep him from drowning. Hollie wouldn't panic, he'd just get soaked. But I couldn't do that to Marie. She would panic for sure, and possibly drown. Boy, I would never take another passenger on my sub again, except rescue victims.

"Will you call? *Please?*"

I felt bad for Marie. It was terrible to be so afraid. I knew that. If it were just me and Hollie I would sit, take my time and really think this through. There was no hurry. We had a couple of days of air in the tanks, at least, that I could pump into the sub as we needed it for breathing. If she could just give me a little time.

"*Please!*"

Marie was going to panic.

"Yes, I will call."

"Oh! Thank you! Thank you! And someone will come, right?"

"Yes, they'll come. I'm floating the antenna now. As soon as it reaches the surface, I'll make the call."

I flipped the switch. A little motor unwound the antenna cable and a small floatation pulled it up quickly. I turned on the short-wave radio. It crackled with static.

"Oh, good!" said Marie.

I put on the earphones and waited for a good connection. I waited. It never came. I could hear Marie outside the earphones. "Are they there?"

"Yes, they're there."

There was no one there. And I knew why. The antenna cable had a maximum capacity of one hundred feet, in the ocean, with little or no current. We were sitting in a river a hundred feet down and the current was pulling the cable sideways. There was no way it would make it even close to the surface. Nobody could hear us. Marie would surely panic when I told her that. I had to think fast. And so, I pretended to make the call. As much as I hated to lie to anybody, I didn't feel I had much choice. When you were trying to rescue a panicking victim in the water, and they climbed on top of you in their panic, thinking somehow that you could save them that way, you were taught to hit them right in the face and knock them out even, if you had to, otherwise they would drown you and both of you would die. Better to give someone a bruise and save their life, and your own.

"Hello? Hello? . . . Yes. This is a vessel under distress . . . a vessel under distress. Yes. . . . submarine . . . a *submarine* . . . domestic submarine . . . in the St. Lawrence River. . . . Yes. . . . We're exactly above the *Empress of Ireland*. Yes, that is correct. . . . Yes. . . . Two persons. . . . Yes. . . . There is a cable wrapped around the propeller. . . . Yes. . . . Forty-eight hours. . . . Yes. Yes, thank you. We will. Thank you very much. Over."

"Oh! Thank you, Alfred! Oh! I'm so glad! So, they're coming?"

"Yes. They're coming."

I went back, climbed onto the bike and tried pedalling backwards and forwards again. Nothing. I hated lying. I really hated it. I promised myself once more that I would never take a passenger on board again. We had designed the sub for only one person. If we could just get through this. I went to the observation window and looked down. And then, something caught my eye.

The weeds that sprung from the wreck were all leaning downstream in the current. The tide had been going out the whole time we were in the area. But now, a few weeds had lost the force of their bend, had straightened, and ever so slowly turned the other way. The tide was reversing. I felt a rush of excitement inside. It was just a hope really, but such an important hope. The tide would reverse the current. The sub would turn. Maybe, just maybe, the cable would loosen in the movement.

Sure enough, all the weeds began to lean in the other direction. The sub began to drift sideways again, very slowly. In my mind I tried to imagine what was happening outside. When was the best time to pedal, as the sub was sliding back, or when it was completely extended in the other direction? I figured the best time to try to pedal would be when the cable was loosest, when the sub was passing directly over the cable.

I stared through the window.

"What are you doing, Alfred?"

"Just a minute."

I watched carefully, trying to judge when we were almost directly over where the cable came out of the wreck. Then, I rushed to the bike, jumped on and tried to pedal backwards. Nothing. Forwards. Nothing. Backwards . . . there was a little movement! Forwards . . . a little more.

Backwards. Suddenly, the driveshaft spun freely. Oh! I could have cried with happiness!

"What? What is it, Alfred? What happened?"

I didn't answer yet. I wanted to see if we were clear of the cable first. I jumped off the bike, rushed to the panel, flipped the switch and pumped air into the tanks. We started to rise. I went back to the window and stared down as we lifted away from the wreck. I watched anxiously, waiting for a sudden halt. There was none. We were completely free of the cable. "Yes! We're free!"

Marie screamed with excitement. In a couple of minutes we were on the surface. She came over hugged me so tightly it hurt.

Chapter 13

WE SURFACED AWASH and I opened the hatch and looked for my first mate. No sign of him. A strong easterly had begun to blow. Now, both wind and current were flowing upstream. I strapped on the harness and climbed out onto the hull, up to my chest in water. How strange it would look to passing sailors to see someone standing in the middle of the river, although the portal was also about a foot out of the water. I hoped Seaweed would spot it soon.

Making my way to the stern, I took a deep breath and went under. I didn't want to spin the propeller until I had a close look to see if there was any damage. Happily, I didn't find any. There was a very small nick where the cable must have been stuck, but that was nothing. The sub was good to go. I was thrilled.

I climbed back inside.

"How does it look?"

"Great! There's no damage. We can leave now."

"You'd better call them, Alfred."

"What?"

"The police. You'd better call them back and tell them we don't need them now. We don't want them to go to all that trouble for nothing."

"Oh! Yah! You're right. I wasn't thinking."

I went to the short-wave and pretended to make the call. Boy, did I ever feel like a phony. That was never going to happen again.

I couldn't get Marie off the sub fast enough. Happily, she felt the same way. We made a beeline towards Rimouski, though I had to sail with the hatch open, the portal just a foot out of water. Marie was unwilling to stay inside the sub if the hatch were shut. And so, in broad daylight, we motored towards a group of sailboats at anchor in twenty feet of water. We wouldn't be difficult to spot if anyone was looking. But there wasn't much I could do about that. The worst thing was to carry an unhappy passenger.

I dropped anchor on the river side of one of the boats that appeared to be empty, inflated the dinghy and paddled Marie to shore. Hollie was very disappointed not to get out for a run, I knew, but I promised him an extra long run that night. He was also sad to see Marie go.

When she climbed onto the beach I could tell she was still carrying her fear. I could see it in her movement. She had been nearly frightened to death. It was an experience that would probably stay with her forever. Personally, I thought she was at greater risk in the kayak with Jacques, a man with a careless attitude towards the water. But fear is not a reasonable thing.

"Alfred. Thank you for rescuing me."

"You're welcome."

"I'm sorry I can't go with you any farther."

"That's okay. I understand. It was not a very nice experience. I'm sorry."

"I'm just too scared."

"I know. It's okay."

"I still wish you would come to Quebec City. I would love to introduce you to my friends. They would really like you. Would you come?"

"Uhh . . . I really should get to Montreal."

She looked sad. "Oh. Just for a short visit? One hour only?"

I knew that was not a good idea, and I should have said so. Why was it so hard to say no? I hated disappointing people. "Umm . . . I guess so. But where would I meet you?"

Her face brightened up and she smiled. "Café la Reine de la nuit. It's in the old city."

"Café what?"

"In English it's called, Queen of the Night Café. Meet me

there Friday night around 11:00, okay? My friends will be there then."

She waved and started up the bank.

I waved back. "Okay! But don't tell them who I am, okay?"

"Okay!"

I paddled back out. We waved one more time and she was gone.

When we returned to the sub, Seaweed was waiting for us. I was so glad to see him.

"Hi, Seaweed! Want some lunch?"

It was three days to Quebec City, three long hot days and short nights. I discovered that this part of Quebec, between Rivière-du-Loup and Quebec City, was one of the most beautiful places in the world. It reminded me of the Mediterranean, except that the water here was darker and colder. Everywhere were beautiful farms next to the water, with cows and colourful houses with sloping roofs and wooden barns and silver churches with needle-like spires. It was so beautiful it was like sailing through a fairytale land.

And there were islands, small ones like the backs of whales and larger ones with houses. The islands were great because they allowed us to moor in the middle of the river and Hollie was able to run around to his heart's content. We even camped there. Each night we made a fire and sat around it. And I learned that dogs and seagulls enjoy staring at a fire just like people do.

Some of the islands had lighthouses that brightened up

the river with narrow beams of light. As pretty as they were, they were there for good reason. The closer we sailed to Quebec City, the narrower and shallower the river became and the more islands we encountered. It would have been next to impossible to navigate without some sort of guide, or, as in our case, sonar. On top of that, there were the tides and currents to consider. I had read in Sheba's book that one early English invasion of Quebec failed when eight ships broke up on rocks in the river and eight hundred and fifty soldiers drowned! Wow! Pretty as the river may be, it would kill you in a flash if you didn't know what you were doing. How unlike sailing on a calm sea, where on occasion you might even fall asleep for a few hours.

As we approached Quebec City, the river became treacherous. There was an archipelago of islands, Archipel de l'Isle-aux-Grues, right in the middle of the river, and a much bigger island, Ile d'Orleans, that was low-lying, very pretty and busy with tourists and picnickers. There were people everywhere. We sailed through the area at periscope depth, which was really a challenge because of the shifting currents and changing depth. I couldn't take my eyes away from the sonar screen. I had read that when the English finally did take Quebec from the French, in 1759, they had to watch the tides closely and time their landing precisely to avoid smashing their boats on the rocks. They came through the fog at night, rowing in long boats, and were challenged by a French soldier on watch. Calling back to him in French, they tricked him into thinking they were French too. That night, they scaled the cliff at the river's edge and attacked the next morning. Who would want to be that soldier?

As the river narrowed, the current flowed faster. It wasn't possible to pass on the north side of Ile d'Orleans because it was too shallow, so, we sailed through the south channel. It was turning dark as we came around the island and the cliffs of Quebec City came into view. The sun was setting just behind the Plains of Abraham, the hilltop where the English and French had fought and where both the English general, Wolfe, and the French general, Montcalm, had been wounded in battle and died. The sunset was pretty, but fiery red. I wondered if Sheba would have thought it an omen.

Chapter 14

THE BEST PLACE to hide is where no one expects you to be.

The river flowed past Quebec at a fast pace and the tide rose and fell an average of ten feet. It was not a place to drop anchor. But the city had lots of marinas, according to the map. The marina closest to the old part of the city had two sections: an inner area for private sailboats, and a more open outer area for larger vessels, which was where, I was guessing, the police kept their rescue vessels.

I was right. After scouting the marina from the river, at periscope depth, I submerged completely, entered the outer section where the police vessels were moored and, opposite them and about two hundred feet away, three barges and a tugboat. Two of the barges were lying side by side and back to front with the other barge and the tugboat. Coming up awash in the pocket between the barges was an excellent place to hide the sub for a few hours in the dark. It was very unlikely there would be people hanging around the police dock at night. And though the marina was well lit, the barges were not, and that made everything a lot easier. Unless you shone a strong light directly on the spot where the portal jutted up just a foot, you would never know there was a submarine there.

I opened the hatch, let Seaweed out, climbed out and lifted myself onto the deck of one of the barges. The coast was clear. I went back for Hollie, sealed the hatch behind us and we made our way onto the pier like nobody's business.

Hollie was such a smart dog. He knew the difference between a beach and a street, and behaved differently on them. And he was an expert at imitating me. If I stopped and looked at things, he would stop and look at things. If I acted cautiously, he would too. Together we strolled down the pier, onto a street, onto another one, over a bridge, across a few more streets, then were swallowed up in a crowd of people enjoying the nightlife of the old city. Even though it was past dark, there were street musicians, performers and artists with easels set up with lights for drawing tourists. There were lots of cafés with tables outside and people eating and drinking on the sidewalks. It was a lovely old city and reminded me of Mallorca, in Spain, from our voyage the year before. No wonder it was so popular.

We walked up and down the steep streets looking for the Café of the Queen of the Night, but I couldn't find it. I didn't mind too much actually; it was just nice to explore the old city. Hollie enjoyed it too. He sniffed at everything, especially other dogs that were chained to poles, gates and fire hydrants. I could tell he didn't understand why the dogs were tied up.

"Don't worry, Hollie. You will never wear a collar or a leash."

Hollie was a sailor, not a pet. He knew it too.

It was almost midnight when we stood in front of an old café with a wooden sign with fancy lettering in French, which I couldn't read, but the sign had the face of a queen. I looked at Hollie. "Maybe this is it."

He wagged his tail. I picked him up and we went in.

There was a small crowd of people sitting around a big table at the back. They were laughing and talking loudly in French. I carried Hollie under my arm and hid him with my jacket. He was used to that when we went inside buildings. Then I saw Marie.

"Alfred!"

She jumped up. The whole group looked in our direction. And then:

"*L'outlaw du sous-marin!* Here he is!"

Everyone stood up and welcomed us to the table. I looked at Marie. I had asked her not to tell anybody who I was. I guess she forgot.

"*Bienvenue! Bienvenue!* Oh! Look! He has got his dog with him! *C'est le chien du sous-marin!*"

Everyone laughed. Marie came over and took Hollie in her arms and hugged him. He didn't mind. He remembered her. One of the men came up to me and sized me up. "I thought you would be much bigger," he said, and laughed.

"*C'est juste un enfant!*" said someone else.

I wasn't sure if I wanted to stay. But Marie begged me to and so I sat down. Someone ordered me a glass of wine but Marie said no, some hot chocolate would be better. And crepes. She was right about that. After a while, Hollie and I were both eating crepes and sipping hot chocolate and water. We sat quietly and listened to the conversation, most of which was in French, so I didn't understand much. But they did ask me a lot of questions and I answered them as well as I could, except for questions about where I was from exactly, or how we built the sub, or, especially, where the sub was right now. Some of the young men kept asking me that but I just smiled and drank my hot chocolate. Before I knew it, it was two o'clock. And then, someone else came in. He stood in front of the table and everyone stopped talking. When Marie looked up and saw who it was, her face went white.

"Jacques!" someone whispered.

My mouth dropped. I didn't know how he could have come from Anticosti Island so quickly. He must have struggled to get here though because he was wearing the same clothes he had worn on the river and they were dirty and smelly. His hair was dirty too and sticking up. He smelled of campfire and the river. He was a mess.

He came over slowly, sweating and breathing heavily, stood in front of Marie and dropped his head. His eyes were bloodshot and I thought maybe he had been crying too. Everyone at the table was silent. I stared at Marie. She wasn't impressed.

"*Je suis tellement désolé. Je te demande pardon.*"

I didn't understand what he was saying but I knew he was asking for forgiveness. You could read it on his face easily enough. I wondered if she would forgive him.

This was a different person than the man I had met on the river. There, he had been so sure of himself, so unconcerned for the conditions and so dangerously mistaken. Now, he looked like a man who realized he had made a big fat mistake and was hoping it was not too late. I wondered if it was too late. Would she forgive him?

As everyone stared I started to feel sorry for him. I mean, I wouldn't trust him on the water, that was for sure, but it was kind of hard not to feel bad for him now. Everyone makes mistakes, Sheba had said.

At first, Marie just looked angry, and I thought maybe Jacques was going to leave empty-handed. He stood and waited patiently, staring at the floor like a little boy who had just broken a window. I knew that feeling. Everyone watched silently, and it was an awkward silence. Hollie looked up at me and he looked awkward too. Eventually Marie's face softened. She reached out her hand and Jacques took it as if it were made of gold. I felt a sudden urge to warn her. Don't trust him! He will do it again. I didn't know why I thought that. What did I know? It wasn't any of my business anyway.

They spoke quietly to each other for a while. Everyone else continued drinking and laughing. Then, Marie and Jacques stood up and announced they were leaving. Jacques was beaming. Marie came over, hugged me and whispered in my ear. "Thank you, Alfred, for everything. Happy travels and keep yourself safe."

She smelled like strawberries. I wanted to warn her not to trust him, but I couldn't. It wasn't my place. She reached down and hugged Hollie. Then she went out the door with Jacques. They never looked back. I realized in a way I didn't really know what forgiveness was all about. I had no experience with it. Though I didn't trust Jacques, I was glad he was getting a second chance.

The rest of the group turned back to laughing and talking. It was time to leave. The sun would be up in just three hours; I didn't want to risk the sub being discovered by an early morning watchman. I stood up and thanked everyone for the hot chocolate and crepes.

"No! No! Stay longer! Tell us more about the river and the sea! Stay!"

I explained that we couldn't, thanked everyone again, waved, and went out the door with Hollie under my arm. Unfortunately, three of the young men followed us. "We just want to have a look at your submarine," they said. "We won't hurt it, we promise."

Rats! This was exactly what I was afraid would happen. They didn't care if I didn't want to reveal the location of the sub or not; they intended to see it. But I didn't trust that they would only look at it. Once they saw it, they'd want to look inside. Then, they'd want to sail it. No. There was no way I would lead them to the sub. And so, late as it was, I headed off in another direction. And they followed.

I put Hollie down and we walked slowly. Hollie was happy. But he kept turning around and looking behind us. He knew we were being followed.

We walked all the way up the hill to the Château Frontenac, around it and over to the Quebec Citadel. I was hoping they would get fed up following us but they didn't. They fell far behind though, and it occurred to me that maybe we could run away from them. But my leg was still too sore to run. Besides, we had already walked so far, and even though Hollie loved to run, he was a very small dog.

And then I thought maybe we could find a way down the cliff. Not a chance! I could better understand now what the English must have gone through the night they scaled the cliff. It was steep!

And so, we turned around and headed back. Now I was tired. The guys following us must have been hiding in the bushes because they disappeared when we turned around, then reappeared later. Boy, were they persistent! Now I was anxious to get back to the sub. The sun would soon be up.

Halfway back I picked Hollie up and carried him. The closer we were to the water, the closer the three guys followed us. All I needed was to get inside with Hollie, shut the hatch and seal it. But I couldn't let them see where the sub was before we were there, or they might jump onto it first and climb inside.

The sky was dark blue when we stepped onto the bridge leading to the police dock. I could see the barges. The young men were following us like three shadows. They reminded me of the ghost I had seen on Anticosti Island, if that's what it had been. What did I know? I was so tired.

I walked slowly and calmly past the police boats. I was half expecting someone to come out of the building there and challenge us. We went a little farther. I put Hollie down. Stopping and turning around, I saw the guys stop too. They were about a hundred and fifty feet away. The sub was still about four hundred feet in front of us. I looked at the small building next to the police boats. I was sure there would be someone there on duty. As the young men passed in front of the building I decided to try something. I opened my mouth and yelled, "Hey! Hey!"

The guys didn't know what was going on. They must have thought I was crazy. But sure enough, a man came out of the building and I heard him ask them what was going on. As they answered him I started walking more quickly. Now we were just three hundred feet from the barges. Now, two hundred. I heard the man yell at me in French. He must have seen us. He kept yelling and I kept walking. I didn't run. I was pretending I didn't hear him. We were just a hundred feet from the barges. A light swung in our direction. It was hand-held because it swung unevenly across the pier. Someone was coming quickly. As soon as we reached the barges, I swept Hollie up and climbed down the ladder. I couldn't see anyone; I was moving too quickly to look. I scampered across the barge and jumped down onto the hull of the sub, startling Seaweed, who had been sleeping there. I opened the hatch and the three of us jumped in. I shut it, sealed it, rushed to the controls and hit the dive switch. Boy, was I relieved!

Chapter 15

WHERE THE ST. LAWRENCE River flows at its narrowest and darkest, just upstream from Quebec City, it flows at its fastest, not counting the rapids west of Montreal. In the retreating tide the river can reach seven knots. Seven knots is about eight miles per hour. A person could walk four miles in an hour if they walked quickly and didn't stop. But they couldn't keep up with the retreating tide by walking. They would have to run.

When the tide flowed in, of course the story was different. Then, the river turned around. But it turned less and less the farther upstream you went. After Quebec City, the river looked like a river proper, no longer like the sea invading the land.

When we left Quebec City, the sky was lit with a flaming sun. A flaming sky at night, went the fisherman's rhyme, and you could expect good weather. A flaming sky in the morning was the one to worry about. I didn't know if Sheba believed in that or not. Ziegfried would probably explain it through scientific fact—the sun passing through particles of evaporation, or something like that—I didn't know, but in the morning came a heavy fog, and with the fog came broken glimpses of a flaming sun, and with that sun came the worst day of my life.

I was so tired. So was the crew. But they could sleep; I had to stay awake watching the sonar screen for rocks and shallows and other vessels. I was sailing by engine with the portal a foot above the surface and the hatch wide open. Occasionally, I would poke my head out the portal and try to scout the surrounding area for a suitable place to sleep, but it seemed almost impossible. When the fog lifted, I planned to submerge and search by periscope. Five miles west of the city the fog was still thick, although it was breaking up in patches here and there. As we approached the village of Saint Nicolas, on the southern shore, the map showed the river running very shallow over a shoal of rock and mud close to shore. Rocks jutted out of the water like peaks on a lemon meringue pie. It was easy enough to avoid them as we motored by, but I heard something that made me hesitate.

It sounded like a cat. How could a cat be so far from shore? That didn't make sense. It sounded so much like a cat wailing its head off that I shut off the engine and drifted for a few minutes, listening carefully.

"Meow, meow, meow, meow . . ."

Yes, it was definitely a cat. It even woke Hollie and brought him to the bottom of the portal. I looked down at him and shrugged my shoulders. "I don't know, Hollie. It must be out there somewhere."

And then, through a break in the fog, I saw it. It was sitting on a rock. How on earth it got there I couldn't imagine. Could it have come out in the low tide, jumping from rock to rock? Maybe it had been drifting on a log and had jumped onto the rock. One thing was certain, when the tide rose, the cat was going to have to swim. And then, it saw us.

"Meow, meow, meow, meow, meow, meow, meow . . ."

It wouldn't stop. I looked down at Hollie. He looked up at me. He looked nervous. "Don't worry, Hollie. That cat is not joining us. I promise."

But I did think I should try to rescue it.

If I hadn't been so tired, if it hadn't been so foggy, if that darn cat hadn't kept meowing constantly, maybe I would have made a better decision about how to rescue it. Maybe.

The tide was going to reverse soon, I knew, but wasn't sure exactly when. This was when the river was most gentle, just before the tide change, and this area of the shoal was particularly easy flowing, as far as I could tell in the fog. But I couldn't bring the sub close to the cat. I could only turn into a cleft in the shoal and tie up to a rock. I made a lasso with rope, threw it onto the rock and pulled it tight—well, after six throws. I didn't drop anchor because I didn't know what the anchor might attach itself to and didn't want to be trying to dive in a seven-knot current later on. It might have been a good idea to inflate the dinghy too, but, as far as I could tell, the shoal appeared shallow enough to cross on foot and the shore was not far away. It really seemed the easiest thing was to pick up the cat and carry it to shore. I thought it would only take a few minutes.

The cat saw me climb out of the sub and jump into the water.

"Meow, meow, meow, meow, meow . . ."

"Yah, yah, I'm coming, I'm coming."

"Meow, meow, meow, meow, meow, meow, meow, meow, meow, meow . . ."

It was really irritating. I was so glad my crew was a dog and a seagull.

A short distance from the sub I climbed onto the shoal, and that brought me standing up to my waist. When I reached the cat, I was up to my chest. Probably I should have gone back for the dinghy then, but the shore was so close, and surely it would get shallower soon.

I took hold of the cat, which wasn't easy because I had to hold it above water and its fur covered my face. And still it meowed! It kept trying to climb on top of my head and it was hard not to get scratched. I made my way towards shore. It did get shallower but I had to watch my step. Several times the rock beneath my feet gave way to mud. I kept turning around to see the sub, which was hard to spot in the foggy air, as it was just the portal jutting up a foot amongst a few scattered rocks. Once or twice I had the impression the sub had shifted its position, but figured that was just my imagination. The fog blocked my view completely a few times but I was almost at the shore. The water was only up to my knees now. The cat never stopped meowing and I felt like throwing it from there, but I thought of Sheba, and how pleased she would be that I had rescued a cat. If we hadn't sailed by, it would have drowned.

I reached the shore finally and put the cat down, but not before it scratched me trying to jump out of my arms. It disappeared the moment it touched ground. What a relief! I turned around. The fog had thickened again. As I started back, I felt uneasy. I should have stretched rope as far as possible towards the shore when I came in, as a guide. I really hadn't thought things through. All I could do now was retrace my steps and look for the same stones. But the fog covered everything. I tried to walk straight out, but once I was just a few steps from shore the fog concealed so much that I couldn't use the shore as a guide. It was important to stay calm, but that uneasy feeling was growing in my stomach. I reached waist depth again, then chest depth and I thought I found the rock where the cat had been, and felt encouraged. I went to waist depth once again and to the end of the shoal. Where was the sub? I felt confused. Which way was the current flowing? Had it changed? Where was the sub?

I searched through the fog. I climbed on rocks and tried to see through it. The river wasn't visible and neither was the shore. What a sickening feeling that was. I didn't even know which way was shore.

"Don't panic!" I told myself.

I made it back to the rock where I had found the cat. Now I was pretty certain the current had turned around. It was stronger now, even in the shallows. I felt a breeze on my face. The wind had picked up with the tide. Maybe it would finally break up the fog. Gradually, it did, and it revealed my worst nightmare. The sub was gone.

Chapter 16

I FELT SICK. I was in shock. When the river turned, it was as if I had been pushing a cart uphill and it suddenly got away from me and was tumbling back down. It would take five and a half hours for the tide to flow out, all of that water rushing back out to sea. The thought of the sub lost in it was too overwhelming for me, and it took me a while to really understand what was happening. For a couple of minutes I just stood there and stared, while the fog continued to break up. I was waiting to see the sub appear. I turned my head from side to side expecting to see it at any moment and realize, oh, that's where I left it.

But that never happened. As the tide went out, the river

began to pick up speed. It pulled the water from the shoal into the current. The river had never filled the shoal completely, and now it was going to empty it. The cat had indeed wandered out in low tide, and if I had left it alone, it would have just walked home the way it came. I might have realized that if I hadn't been so tired.

I broke my trance and jumped into action. Although the sub had been swept away, it wouldn't have travelled far yet. I crouched down and looked carefully down the surface of the river for any rises but couldn't see much through the fog patches. Had the sub gone completely under? Different images raced through my head. Probably what happened was that the current pulled the sub sideways and tilted it because it was tied to the rock. As it tilted, water spilled inside. Then, the rope slipped from the rock and the sub started to drift. As soon as the sensors on the floor picked up water rushing in, the hatch shut and sealed automatically. Hollie and Seaweed had gotten wet but were fine. I felt certain this was what happened, exactly like that.

I jumped into the water and began to swim downstream. It was a desperate thing to do but I felt that the sub wasn't far away, and maybe with a little luck I would find it. It didn't take long to realize what a foolish idea that was. The current was so strong I could hardly even swim with it; it just pulled me where it wanted me to go. And I was so busy fighting it I couldn't look for the sub.

"Come on!" I yelled to myself. "Find it!"

With a lot of effort I managed to get back to the rocky shallows, pull myself up and make my way to shore. It was exhausting. But at least I was on dry land now. I could run along the bank and try to spot the sub.

That was very hard and very discouraging. Not only was the fog hanging around still, but the sky had darkened. It was going to rain. And though I was on the beach, there was no road beside the water. Farther east there was. I had seen it. But for now, I had to run along the rocky shore, and sometimes amongst trees and bushes.

And then, I thought I saw it. I wasn't sure, but I thought I did. The water that poured into the sub must have pulled it down, and then, after the sump pumps removed that water, it rose again, but not quite to where it had been. There was also the current to account for. It could easily make the difference of a foot or so in the sub's buoyancy. In any case, I thought I caught a glimpse of the top of the hatch in the growing choppiness. And if I had, I had an idea of how fast it was moving. I would have to run to keep up.

Inside the sub Hollie and Seaweed would be fine. I knew they would be sitting on their spots, well, except that Hollie's blanket would be all wet, and Seaweed probably had hopped onto my cot. Hollie would be on it too, if the water had reached that far, but I couldn't imagine it had. He could have climbed onto my seat though, or the bicycle seat. Hollie was a very smart dog and he was a survivor. The bigger danger was that the sub would collide with another vessel, especially one sailing upriver, especially a large one, like a freighter, that would not be able to turn quickly and would assume that the vessel heading towards it would swerve first. That was my biggest fear.

The only thing going in our favour at the moment was the fact that we had been sailing so close to the south side of the river, at least a mile from the main traffic area. But that would change when the sub approached the city once again, five miles downstream, where the river narrowed briefly to just half a mile wide at the bridges. Then, it narrowed once again at Levis, six miles farther downstream, then veered north a tiny way, then split in two, with the sailable part of the river making a very sharp right turn and the rest of it flowing straight on into the shallows north of Isle-de-Orleans. The sub would never make that turn on its own. It would drift north until it struck bottom somewhere in the shallows and would be exposed in the low tide. But that's only if it didn't collide with another vessel along the way.

I ran along the shore and climbed over rocks and mud and went up and down hills and around tiny inlets but never caught another glimpse of the sub. Then, I found an old buoy. Running into the water as far as I could, I threw the buoy with all my might. The river grabbed it and pulled it along. Now I had something with which to gauge the speed of the current. Now I would be able to tell if I were keeping up with it.

I wasn't! The shore was twisting around too much and it

was too hard to run fast enough. I was growing more exhausted and feeling sicker in my stomach all the time. There had to be another way.

I reached a small road that ran alongside the river. The buoy was out of my sight now. Along the road were a few houses. Between two houses I saw a fence. Leaning against the fence was a bicycle.

I had never stolen anything in my whole life. I stared at the door of the house. It didn't look like anyone was home. I thought it over quickly. I could run to the door and bang on it and wait for the owner to come out. Then, they might speak English and they might not. I would have to explain to them that I needed to borrow their bicycle but would bring it back. Why did I need it? To catch up with my submarine. Who was going to believe that?

I ran across the yard, grabbed the bicycle and jumped on it. As I rode out of the yard I heard someone come out of the house and yell after me. They chased me into the road and continued yelling. It was the first time I truly *felt* like an outlaw. Even then, I promised myself I would return the bicycle if I could. The truth was: I would do anything to save Hollie and Seaweed.

I raced down the street as fast as I could, and I *was* fast on the bike because of all the pedalling I did in the sub. My legs were very strong and I could pedal for hours if I had to, even when I was tired. But I was expecting somebody to come chasing me with a car. And they did. I also expected the road to swing away from the river and it did. But that worked in my favour because I kept going straight, right across the fields and through a wooded area, until I reached another street. There were little pockets of neighborhoods here and there, then nothing between but fields and woods. But eventually the road veered closer to the river. That's where I knew they might catch me. They would call the police for sure. I was hoping to reach the bridges first. If I could get onto one of the bridges, I'd be able to spot the sub drifting below.

Two bridges crossed the St. Lawrence River at Quebec City. They lay side by side at the narrowest point in the river, just west of the city. I had seen them just that morning on our way up the river. The one on the downstream side was older, one of those big iron trestle bridges that you can see for miles and miles. The other one was just a long, flat concrete slab. Both were high above the river, too high for a person to jump from without getting killed. But the trestle bridge had iron arches that curved downward into the water. I had seen them clearly enough, even through the fog, and figured it was possible to climb down to a height from which I could jump without getting killed. I mean, it would be dangerous but it was possible.

I reached the road beside the river and I saw the buoy! Farther down the river the trestle bridge was barely visible. The sky was darkening and the fog was turning to heavier mist. I could feel it was going to rain.

I knew I was pedalling faster than the current because I passed the buoy easily. The sub couldn't be more than half a mile ahead of that. If I could just reach the bridge, I'd have time to see it pass beneath. Then I could climb down the arches, jump into the water, regain the sub and rescue my crew. It was a good plan. And then, I heard a siren.

The road followed the river until the last two miles or so, when it veered to avoid a wooded area. I saw a trail enter the woods and I took it. As I disappeared into the trees I turned around and saw the lights of a police car on the road. Yikes! Had they seen me?

Where the trail came out of the woods was another neighbourhood with lots of streets and houses. I pedalled as close to the river as possible. The bridges were closer now. So was the wail of the police siren. They must have seen me enter the woods and guessed where I'd come out. If they caught me they would surely arrest me, and I'd go to jail, or at least some sort of correctional centre. I tried not to think about it. Nothing was going to stop me from trying to rescue Hollie and Seaweed.

The police car was racing through the neighbourhood. Sometimes its siren grew louder and sometimes fainter. They were searching for me. Probably they just thought I was trying to hide. Luckily they didn't know where I was heading. I decided that if they saw me now, where they could easily catch me, I would race to the river and jump in. They would have to call rescue boats then, and that would take a while, and that would buy me some time. But my chances of finding the sub like that were pretty slim. I needed to get onto the bridge.

As I came to the very end of the last neighbourhood before the bridge, and rode to the end of the last street, I saw the police car pass in the other direction just one street up and heard its engine race after we passed each other. They had seen me. But they had to reach the end of that street, turn down one block and race up the street I had just crossed. That would take them at least half a minute. I raced onto the grass that led to the last wooded area. I jumped off and ran with the bike through the trees, where I found a dirt road. I climbed back on the bike and followed the road down and around and under the first bridge. I heard the siren again. The dirt road continued to the second bridge, the trestle bridge, and ended there. I jumped off the bike and ran up the hill to where the highway went onto the bridge. It was a steep hill and I was so out of breath my lungs were burning. But I couldn't allow them to catch me now.

It was raining when I climbed onto the bridge. There was a sidewalk there and a metal fence to keep people from falling, or jumping, I supposed. As I ran up the sidewalk my lungs and throat were burning. I looked down to where I had left the bike. The police car was there, its lights flashing, and a policeman was looking up in my direction. And he saw me.

As I raced up the sidewalk, trying to gauge how far from shore I was at each step, I remembered what Ziegfried had said about jumping into water from a height. From a couple of hundred feet, he had said, hitting the surface of the water was like hitting concrete. If you could hold your body perfectly straight and enter like a needle, you might survive. But it was extremely unlikely. If you landed flat, you would break every bone in your body.

Well, I had no intention of jumping from such a height. I would climb over the fence, scale down one of the arches and jump from a reasonable height.

The rain picked up and so did the wind. When I reached over and dug my fingers into the wire mesh of the bridge fence, a strange thought ran through my head. Was this what my life had come to, a fugitive running from the law? Was this what I was now? No, I told myself. No. This was not who I was. This was not what I had become. This was just a nightmare. As soon as this was over and I had regained my submarine, I would sail straight out to sea. I would get off this river and never come back. I would live my life without ever meeting my father. So what? I could live with unfinished business. Who really cares about that?

Heights, I had learned, always look worse from above. From below, they're not such a big deal. Even that morning, as we had passed beneath the bridge, I remembered looking up and admiring its size but didn't imagine it was as high as it appeared now. As I climbed over the fence onto a metal girder, I found the height terrifying. And I found shimmying down the girder terrifying, because there was no railing there, and the metal was wet and slippery and the wind tugged at me. But there were police sirens on the bridge, coming from both directions. There was no going back now.

As I shimmied down, I looked hard for any sign of the sub. The height was dizzying. I felt sick. I was afraid of falling.

"Just get closer!" I told myself.

I reached a kind of landing and felt safer there. The wind was starting to howl. I couldn't tell if the sirens were still wailing or not. No one would come down after me, I was certain about that, but they would call for rescue boats. I shimmied down farther. The height was not so terrifying now but it was still dangerous. Where was the sub? How long before it would pass beneath? I shimmied farther. Once, I almost lost my grip and it scared me to death. I fought back the urge to break down and cry. Instead, I turned and looked at the river and yelled at it with all my might:

"GIVE ME BACK MY SUBMARINE!"

I saw a shadow in the water below. I heard a man yell from a megaphone above. Taking a deep breath, I jumped.

Chapter 17

I HIT THE WATER so much harder than I expected. It was what I imagined being hit by a car would feel like. The force ripped the sneakers from my feet. It would leave me with bruises on my back and legs, but I would deal with that later.

When I rose to the surface I was dizzy and could hardly see straight. It was raining harder now and very windy. Visibility was still poor. Once again I found it impossible to swim in the current; it was so much work just to stay afloat. But where was the sub? I swung my head around and could hardly see the bridge through the rain. It loomed above me like a dark shadow; the river was pulling me away quickly. I tried to look downriver. If rescue boats were coming, I couldn't see them. Surely they wouldn't come so quickly? Where, I wondered desperately, was the sub? I had to find it, I just had to. But I couldn't see anything. Everything was fuzzy. And then, something appeared above me. How was that possible? It looked like an angel. Was it an angel? Was this what Sheba's dream had been about? I was so confused.

I wiped my eyes and looked up at the wings flapping above me. My heart glowed. It was Seaweed. Oh my heavens, how wonderful to see him! He must have jumped from the sub before the hatch shut. Here he was, hovering in the air above me. He must have been wondering what the heck I was doing.

"Seaweed! Show me where the sub is! Show me the sub!"

He continued to flap his wings and hover above me. I thought of something else.

"Go find Hollie, Seaweed! Find Hollie!"

He raised himself higher in the air and flew a short distance away. I watched him land and could tell by the way he was sitting on the river that he was actually standing on something. The hatch!

I could swim underwater better than on the surface because that's what I had trained myself to do. I took a deep breath, went under and swam as hard as I could across the current. I swam and swam, came up for air and went back under. The water was too dark to see through but when I came up for air I caught sight of Seaweed and corrected my direction. In a few minutes my hand struck the hard shell of the hull. I was so happy I could have cried. I think I did actually.

The top of the portal was level with the surface of the river. It jutted up a few inches then went under again. I found a handle, pulled myself over and opened the hatch. Water spilled inside, down on top of Hollie, who was staring up and barking excitedly. He scrambled out of the way. Seaweed dropped out of the air, landed on the edge of the open hatch and peered inside, uncertain whether or not to go in.

"Biscuits, Seaweed!" I said anxiously. "Biscuits!"

He looked at me sideways, questioning my sincerity. I said it again, more confidently. "Biscuits!"

He dropped inside. I pulled myself in after him, with lots of water, sealed the hatch, rushed to the control panel and flipped the dive switch.

We went down to periscope depth. I picked up Hollie and hugged him. He was very excited but perfectly okay. I scanned the radar screen. Three small boats were rushing towards our area. They were coming to rescue the young man who had just jumped from the bridge. I wished I could have explained to them that I was okay, but didn't want to expose the sub. Maybe when they didn't find a body they would figure that I had swum to safety. Or maybe they would assume the river had claimed another victim. Not this time. I checked the depth, dove to fifty feet, engaged the batteries and headed downstream.

My only thought was to get away. This river was far too dangerous. I didn't want to disappoint Sheba but maybe Marie was right. Maybe the whole river was cursed. Look at all the people who had died on it. Sheba wouldn't want me to die trying to find my father.

But I was too tired to go anywhere yet. Being tired was exactly how I had made the worst mistakes. I couldn't afford to make any more. So, I motored back to the police marina, snuck in under the barges to the very same spot, but didn't raise the portal above the surface. If anyone started the engine on the tugboat, I knew I would hear it loud and clearly. I shut everything off, fed the crew and got ready for bed.

Hollie's blanket was soaked. I wrung it out, hung it up and put my jacket down for him. I knew my jacket was the only thing that would substitute for his blanket because he was used to sleeping on it inside buildings. Seaweed was tired and went straight to sleep. I peeled off my wet clothes and examined my bruises. It felt like somebody had beaten me up. My leg was still sore from getting trapped in the wreck. The river was trying to kill me! Sheba's last prediction was that something terrible would happen on our way, but that we would be okay. I thought it had already happened at Anticosti Island but this was worse. This was the worst thing that had ever happened to me. I was done with this river. It wasn't worth it. Never before in my life had so many things gone wrong.

As I pulled on dry clothes and lay down on my cot, I

heard Hollie paw my jacket into an acceptable shape. It took him a long time but he plopped down finally and sighed. Things could have turned out so differently, I knew, and I shivered in my bed just thinking about it. I felt grateful I was still alive. I felt grateful my crew was all right. Ever so slowly, I fell asleep.

We slept a long time and I had long, interesting dreams. In one dream there was an angel, but I couldn't see her. I asked her if she was the angel of the river and she said yes. I asked her if I would ever see her. She said that I already knew who she was. I thought that was a strange answer and felt the strangeness of it still when I woke.

After tea and breakfast with the crew I started to feel better. With the lights on and all of us rested, everything seemed different again. The river was very dangerous, that was for sure. Many people had been killed by it, for hundreds of years. But I didn't believe in the curse of the mummy. I still wasn't sure if I believed in ghosts. I had been trapped by the old wreck because I had thrown the anchor without looking first. I had lost the sub in the river because I had abandoned it carelessly to save a cat. Those were mistakes in judgment, to tell the truth. Jacques Cartier had travelled up the river successfully. Why couldn't I? Surely he had had difficult moments? Surely he must have felt discouraged at times? I read that he ran into storms in the mouth of the river and had to change course and seek shelter. He also fired a cannon to scare the local people when he was unsure of their intentions. He didn't trust them. He must have felt afraid then, and yet he never gave up and never let the river beat him. He had used good judgment. As I drank my tea, peeled some oranges and studied the map, I decided not to let the river beat me either. I didn't believe in curses and I just hated giving up.

The rescue boats had returned. I felt bad they had searched for me, although that was their job, and it *was* good practice. Rescuers had to practise to stay sharp. There would be no dredging of the river with a current of seven knots. There would be no point. There would be no extensive searching either. They would know that a body would wash up downstream. I bet there were places where bodies got caught in the shallows and the police knew just where to look for them. I read in Sheba's book that Hindus in India would burn bodies instead of burying them, then put the ashes in the Ganges River, which they believed was a god, then let the river carry them away. But sometimes they couldn't afford to burn the whole body and would just drop the charred remains into the water. And there were crocodiles in the Ganges. Yikes! I was glad there were no crocodiles in the St. Lawrence.

It was early dawn. Today there was no flaming sun. I waited for a freighter to pass by the front of the marina. She was sailing to Montreal, or perhaps to the Great Lakes through the St. Lawrence Seaway. Giving her a quarter-mile lead, I motored out at periscope depth and settled in her wake. How smart to follow a ship that had likely navigated the river a hundred times. Why hadn't I thought of that before?

Chapter 18

TWENTY-FOUR HOURS to Montreal. We slipped in behind the freighter and stayed in her wake the whole way. I felt like a camel driver. Staying awake on a camel all day is a hard job. I learned that a year ago when we visited North Africa. So is following a freighter up a river. I made lots of tea, kept the radio on, and, after dark, sailed on the surface with the hatch open. But it was painful staying awake so long. Sailing up the river was the hardest thing I ever did.

Hollie was restless too. It had been two days since he was out for a run. He stood in the portal with me as we plowed upriver with lots of lights around. The sky had cleared and the stars were out. Hollie had an appreciation for the stars.

He was quiet about it, but I could tell he felt an awe when he looked up and saw a sea of lights above us, because the stars were always more spectacular at sea, and, well, even on the river.

But things became complicated as we approached the city. Up to Trois-Rivières, about halfway, it was easy. Then, the river spread into a lake for twenty miles or so, Lac St. Pierre. That was easy too. But the far side of the lake shattered into fragments of a river, like ice breaking up, and, although the map showed the best way to go, I was glad that freighter was in front of us. As she disappeared between two narrow riverbanks, like a moose disappearing into the woods, I submerged to periscope depth, closed the distance between us to an eighth of a mile and followed her in.

The sun was breaking as we entered Montreal's east side. I was shaking my head now to keep awake. There were islands, pieces of islands and slivers of river in all directions. It looked more like an estuary than a river. Nothing about the St. Lawrence was what I had expected it to be.

Hollie was dying to get out and run, and there was no way he would settle for a day's sleep, especially when Seaweed had just woken, yawned, stretched his wings and demanded to be let out. Seaweed didn't take no for an answer. He tapped his beak on the bottom rung of the ladder and glared at me. So, I surfaced awash, opened the hatch and out he went. I supposed I needed to turn my sleep around again anyway if I were going to go looking for somebody.

The lights of the city shone brilliantly in the early morning: houses, more houses and endless buildings. Right in front of us was Ile Ste-Thérèse, an island of farms, which looked a bit out of place in a big city. The farms ran to the water's edge where there was a small beach. The water was shallow. On the north-east side of the island, in a pool with little current, I dropped anchor, inflated the dinghy and rowed Hollie to shore. We didn't go far. If anyone saw us so early in the morning we'd rush back to the sub and take off.

Hollie hit the sand running. I think he liked the feeling of somersaulting. He bolted back and forth, then stopped in front of me and stared up with eyes like a crazy person.

"You're crazy, Hollie!"

And he was off again. What a wild mutt!

I sat on the beach and kept an eye on the sub. The river wasn't like the sea at all. It was much more unpredictable. I would never turn my back on it again.

While Hollie ran, I sat. I was stiff. My back was sore and so were my legs. I was so tired I could have slept for a month. The thought of looking for my father was bugging me too. Where would I begin? I knew he probably worked on the dockyards still, so I figured I could start there. But the dockyards of Montreal were enormous. I thought maybe I could ask about him at an employment office, if I could find one. I could look him up in the phone book too. Russell Pynsent. But I didn't want to call. I'd rather find him first and have a look at him before I actually spoke to him. And I didn't want anyone to know who *I* was, or that I was even looking for my father. So, I decided to use my grandfather's last name, Peddle, the same as my mother's, instead of my own.

After Hollie had run himself silly, he ran around sensibly. Then he ran in spurts and starts. Finally, he came over and stood in front of me, panting.

"Had enough? Can we go now? I'm exhausted."

He dropped his head, his way of shrugging in agreement.

"Don't worry. You're going to get a *lot* of exercise tomorrow. You'll see."

But where to hide the sub in Montreal? We needed to find a pocket of water somewhere without current of any kind. And it had to be hidden. And I had to be able to come and go because I'd need to return to sleep. And it had to be visible to Seaweed, so he would stay in the area. What a tall order! All I needed at the moment was a place to sleep for the day. In the night I would search for a better place.

We paddled back to the sub, deflated the dinghy and climbed inside. I never knew if anyone was watching. It was unlikely. Just because you couldn't see anybody didn't mean nobody was watching. Once we were submerged, we were pretty much impossible to find, even in a river. I loved that.

After Ile Ste-Thérèse, we passed Ile de la Commune and Ile Sainte-Marguerite. There were so many islands in the river! Then, on the starboard side I spied a large container terminal. Big dockyards were good places to hide. We sneaked along the industrial zone with our periscope up just like any other iron bar jutting out of the water, except that ours was moving. And I found a spot.

In front of a row of huge grain elevators, with gigantic arms raised for pouring grain into the bellies of ships, there was a long, narrow, concrete breakwater. At its base was a tiny cove that must have been created when they sank rocks for the breakwater. It was only big enough for the sub, but I could tie up there and we would be hidden by the concrete wall. Sitting like a stone in a puddle at the very edge of the industrial zone, its portal showing a foot above the surface, the sub was practically invisible from the water and land.

I fed Seaweed and wished him a good day. He would stay out and mingle with the local birds and keep watch on the sub. Ziegfried said that Seaweed was a gregarious seagull. That meant that he liked to party. Hollie and I were more like hermits, although Hollie loved attention and loved to have his fur brushed. If I had fur I probably would have enjoyed that too. I fed Hollie, dimmed the lights, climbed into bed and drifted off to sleep before he even finished chewing.

I woke from disturbing dreams, having slept away the whole afternoon and night. It was early morning—I'd missed my chance to move the sub. Why was I really looking for my father anyway? Was I hoping he would become part of my life now? No. I wasn't. Did I hope maybe he would start writing to me and send me things? No. Was I curious about him, what he looked like and how he behaved? Maybe a little. Was he a nice person? Was I afraid that maybe he wasn't, that maybe he was somebody I wouldn't like? Was I afraid that he would get involved in my life and try to stop me from exploring?

Yes.

Hollie came over, wagging his tail. I reached down and patted his ear with my toe.

"Hi, buddy. We need a bag for you."

He looked confused.

"I think I'll empty the tool bag. It has a shoulder strap and a mesh top. You'll be able to breathe and look outside. No one will see you."

He looked as if he were thinking it over.

"It's a good idea. We're going to walk forever."

He wagged his tail at that.

"Yah. We're going to look for somebody. But we might not find him."

I climbed down from my cot and put the kettle on. Hollie followed closely. He still looked confused.

"Don't worry. It's okay if we don't find him."

Chapter 19

HIDING THE SUB was one thing, crossing the industrial zone on foot was another. Hollie didn't want to go inside the tool bag. I understood that, but he really had to. Somebody walking through the dockyard might raise suspicion; somebody walking a dog definitely would. But try telling that to a dog who's excited about getting out for a walk.

The tool bag was perfect for carrying him. It was really just a box made of tough nylon, with a wooden bottom and a mesh top. It was big enough for him to stretch out, turn around, eat snacks and sleep. Hollie weighed twelve pounds. The tool bag weighed about seven, so it was a lot to carry around all day, especially when I was also carrying water and snacks. But the bag had a wide strap and hung comfortably over my shoulder and swung against my back. I could run with it if I had to, but not as fast as I could without it. Hollie was not pleased when I put him in the bag, and he furrowed his brow at me, but I promised him he would get out as soon as we got away from the grain elevator pier. I felt like telling him that *I* was the captain, but didn't think he would appreciate that very much.

We climbed out of the sub and greeted Seaweed, who was sitting on the concrete wall above us. I tossed him some dog biscuits. He stayed behind when I climbed onto the road along the pier and started walking. Seagulls would make perfect spies. They can go anywhere and hang around all day if they want to and nobody ever suspects them of anything.

The road ran along a giant open space, like an enormous parking lot, except that there weren't any cars in it. There wasn't anything in it. Maybe it was a spare lot for stacking containers when the regular lots were full. It would be a lot easier to cross at night, although there was a gate at the far side, and we had to pass through that. Maybe we'd just find my father today, say hello, come back and leave tonight. Yes, well, I knew it wasn't going to be that easy.

We walked all the way across the lot, past the grain elevators, towards the gate. I slipped through the gate, squeezing between two metal poles and pulling Hollie after me. Then, an orange truck stopped and a man called out to me.

He called in French, then in English.

"Hey! You're not supposed to be here. What are you look-ing for?"

I approached the truck looking as innocent as I could. "Can you tell me where the employment office is?"

"The employment office?"

"Yes."

"What employment office?"

"For the dockyards."

"For the . . . what are you looking for, to work on the docks?"

He looked me over.

"Yes."

"How old are you?"

"Sixteen."

"Sixteen? So, you're looking for a summer job then?"

"Yes."

"Well, you're in the wrong area altogether. You don't come down here looking for work, kid."

"You don't?"

"No. You got to go to an employment office . . . in the city."

"Where's that?"

He rolled his eyes at me. Sheba said that rolling your eyes at somebody was a sign of contempt. That meant he didn't like me.

"There are lots of employment offices. You'll have to find that yourself, but you won't find it here. Now, you'd better move along. You're not supposed to be here."

"Oh. Okay."

From the grain terminal I crossed the train tracks and took another street that bordered a neighbourhood with houses. Once we were beyond the train tracks I let Hollie out. He looked up and down the street, probably looking for a beach.

"Nope. No beach today, Hollie. City walk today."

Oh, well. He settled into a nice trot beside me and smelled everything. In the city he could teach other dogs how to behave.

We found a phone booth and I flipped through the white pages but couldn't find Russell Pynsent. I didn't want to call anyway. I flipped through the yellow pages, then the blue pages, then the grey pages, until I found what I thought was an employment office. I dialed the number. Someone answered in French, but spoke English when I did.

"Permanent or temporary?"

"Umm . . . temporary."

"Skilled or labour?"

"I'm not sure."

"How much education do you have?"

"Umm . . . grade eight."

"Labour. We have a temporary labour employment office on Rue Sherbrooke Est. Do you know where that is?"

"I can find it."

She gave me the address and I wrote it down.

"Thank you."

"You're welcome."

She sounded tired and bored. I wouldn't want her job.

Rue Sherbrooke Est was two miles away. Half an hour of brisk walking. When we reached the street, we had to turn west. Hollie was staring at the tool bag now. You can only smell so much concrete.

I found the employment office when I spotted a group of men hanging around on the sidewalk outside a small unattractive building. The men were smoking and laughing and spitting on the ground. They looked more like hobos to me than workers. They looked like they slept outside. I wondered if they did. They stopped talking when they saw me come over and enter the building.

Inside were about twenty men who looked more or less the same. I was by far the youngest one there, and they looked at me kind of suspiciously. I went up to the counter, waited for my turn and said I was looking for work.

"How old are you?"

"Sixteen."

The man behind the counter nodded his head and handed me a sheet of paper and a pen.

"Fill this out."

He spoke to me respectfully and didn't roll his eyes. I was glad about that. I took a seat beside another guy filling out the form. It asked for my name, address, telephone number, allergies, experience, whether or not I had ever made an insurance claim on a job site before, and my social insurance number. All I could write truthfully was my experience, that I had no allergies and never made a claim. For my name I wrote, Alfred Peddle. For the address, I wrote, Rue Sherbrooke E., and made up a number. I looked at the form of the guy beside me and copied his phone number and social insurance number then changed them a little bit. I was only planning to work for a day or two to get information to help me find my father. I wasn't even expecting to get paid.

When I stood at the counter again and handed in my form, the man read it over, made a strange face and stared at me. Shoot! He must have known I was making it all up.

"Says here, you can sharpen tools."

That part was true. I tried to sound bored. "Yah."

"That's a skill."

"Oh."

He read some more. "Says here, you can clean engines. Are you a mechanic?"

"No."

"But you can clean engines?"

"Yes."

"That's a skill."

"Oh."

"You're a skilled labourer."

Some of the other men looked up at me.

"Oh. Well, I worked in a machine shop for a few years."

That was true too.

"And you're sixteen?"

"Yah."

"And you wanna work at the dockyards?"

"Yes."

"How come you wanna work at the dockyards?"

"I don't know; I just like the water."

He stared at me closely. I tried to look disinterested, as if I didn't really care if I got the job or not. He flipped through a binder with loose pages and spoke as he did it. "You can sharpen tools and clean engines. You better be able to do that if I send you down to a machine shop."

"I can."

"Okay. Here you go. It starts at twelve-fifty an hour. It's only six hours a day and it's temporary. But if they like you they might keep you. Come back here to get paid."

"How often?"

He squinted at me. "Every day."

He took a sheet of paper, wrote down the address, drew a quick map and handed it to me.

"When do I start?"

"Yesterday."

He turned his attention to somebody else.

"Thank you."

He never answered. I looked around the room at the men staring at me. I never knew I was a skilled worker.

Chapter 20

THE MACHINE SHOP was in a corner of a long building that sat on a pier. I had to show the paper I was carrying to be allowed through a gate into the area. If I got hired, they would give me a card with my name on it and I would have to use that to go in and out. I had let Hollie walk on the way down so that he was good and tired and was happy to sleep in the bag for the rest of the day.

As I pulled open a heavy metal door and stood in the doorway, I heard the whir of industrial machines, and, above them, the scream of a motor that needed oil. Metal spinning against metal at high speeds, without sufficient lubrication, could sound like raccoons fighting at night. It was a disturbing sound, and yet, if you were working right beside it all day, you might not even notice it. I was met by a burly man who looked like he believed I didn't belong there.

"What do you want?"

I tried to look bored and handed him the paper without saying anything. He squinted at the paper and got it all dirty with the grease on his hands. "What's this?"

I cleared my throat and considered spitting out the door but didn't think I could do it convincingly enough. I didn't want to look like an amateur spitting.

"We don't need anybody. Why'd they send you here? Must be a mistake."

Rats. I knew it wasn't going to be easy. He handed back the paper. "They made a mistake, kid. Go somewheres else."

I took the paper, looked at the address again, then stared at the address on the door. It was the right address. We stood and stared at each other for a minute. I had the feeling that maybe he was waiting for me to say something to prove myself. I took a shot at it.

"Your grinder needs oil."

"What?"

He sounded insulted.

"Your grinder. It needs oil. Sounds like somebody's killing a baby."

He grinned. "Does it now? And how the heck would you know it's the grinder?"

"'Cause it's sitting beside the lathe and it can't be the lathe."

"Is that right? And why can't it be the lathe?"

"'Cause nobody would forget to oil the lathe. And if it were the lathe, it would sound like a hundred babies were being killed."

His grin opened up into a laugh and I saw a row of yellow teeth. He grabbed the paper out of my hand and read it again. "Can you really sharpen tools?"

"Yup."

He looked up at me again. It wasn't a look of respect, but he didn't roll his eyes either. "Follow me."

I followed him through the noisy workshop, down a hallway to a door on one side. It was just a large closet. He swung the door open, clicked on the light and stepped inside. There was dust everywhere. There were tool cabinets, benches with vice grips, and, on one wall, about two dozen saws hanging. There were cross-cutters and rip-saws, short and long-toothed, coarse and fine, long and short. At a glance they all had one thing in common: they were dull. As we stood and stared at the saws, an old man in janitor overalls passed by the door.

"Hey! Jacob!"

The old man stopped and entered the room. He had white hair and a sparkle in his eyes. He looked friendly.

"Yah, boss?"

"When's the last time these saws were sharpened?"

It sounded like an accusation more than a question.

"Hmmm. How long have I been working here?"

Jacob looked at me and winked.

"Seventeen years," said the boss.

"Oh. Ummm . . . seventeen years ago."

The boss turned to me. "Sharpen them."

"All of them?"

"All of them!"

He went out the door. I wanted to ask where the files were. Jacob read my mind. "You'll find the files in the drawer." And then he said something that showed he was paying a lot more attention than you'd think. "Sweet dog. Keep him quiet."

I put Hollie down where he could see me. Then I climbed up on the bench, reached up and forced open a small dirty window to let in some fresh air. It had probably never been opened before. I pulled the first saw down from the wall, searched the drawers for the files, then settled comfortably on the chair and started to work. Through the mesh I saw Hollie watch me curiously, sigh, roll around a few times, plop down and go to sleep.

A few hours later I had three saws sharpened. The boss stepped into the doorway and watched me file. He was holding a four-by-six block of wood in one hand.

"How many'd you do?"

"Three."

"Lemme see."

He came in, picked up a long cross-cut saw, fastened the block of wood in a vice, dropped the saw onto it, took a breath and began to cut the wood. The saw fell through the wood like butter. The boss smiled, but not at me. He put the saw down and went out the door without a word. I took a sandwich out of my jacket pocket, took a bite and gave Hollie a bite. This was my first paying job. Cool.

In the afternoon, when everyone was leaving the shop, everyone except Jacob, who looked like he lived there, I went to him and asked him if he had ever heard of a man called Russell Pynsent.

"I don't remember so. Does he come from Newfoundland too?"

"How did you know I was from Newfoundland?"

His eyes sparkled a little like Sheba's. "Oh, you can just tell. Now, if you were from New Orleans, or Boston, I'd be able to tell that too. It's the way you speak."

"Oh."

"Pynsent, you say? So . . . you must be a Pynsent too, I gather."

"Ummm . . . no. Peddle."

"Oh. And why would you be looking for this Russell Pynsent fella?"

"No reason."

"Mmmhmm."

Jacob made a serious face and looked as if he understood perfectly. I was pretty sure he could read my mind.

"Got a place to stay, have you?"

"Yup."

"And I figure *he* travels with you?"

He nodded towards Hollie, who was awake and standing in the tool bag on my back.

"Yup."

Jacob scratched his head with one hand. The other hand was wrapped around the handle of a wide-bottomed broom. "I live here. Got a room in the back. Fridge and TV too. There's always room on the floor if a young fella is stuck for a place to stay. I've seen worse places."

"I'm great. Thanks."

I wasn't about to tell him I lived in a submarine.

"Sure enough. There's quite a few machine shops on the dockyards. Ask around."

"Thank you. I will."

Hollie was happy to get out again, even on concrete. We walked back to the employment office, which took about an hour. Hollie was ready for the bag by then. I entered the room again, not knowing what to expect. Would they have discovered that my information was all made up and tell me to get lost? Would they have called the police? Probably not. I went up to the counter and waited.

"Peddle?"

"Yes."

"Here. Be there tomorrow at ten sharp. Don't be late."

He handed me an envelope.

"Thanks."

He never answered. I went to the door and opened the envelope. There was money inside. Fifty-five dollars and one quarter. They had kept some money for unemployment insurance and other fees.

"Peddle!" yelled the man at the counter. Rats! Now they've figured out I am an imposter. I turned.

"Yes?"

"What size are your feet?"

"What? Oh. Ten."

He reached behind him, lifted up a pair of old steel-toed work-boots and dropped them onto the counter with a loud thud. "Wear these on the job. It's the law."

I went back and picked them up. "Got it."

I didn't say thank you this time. I caught his eye for a second and thought he almost smiled. And I went out.

Outside, the street was filled with the noise of the city. Cars, busses and people rushed by. I felt strangely happy. There was something magical about receiving money for a day's work. I couldn't quite get my head around it. I enjoyed sharpening tools. It was something Ziegfried had taught me and he was a good teacher. It seemed strange that someone would pay me money to do it. Tomorrow I would make even more money. Cool.

Chapter 21

HOLLIE AND I WERE starving. So, we went into a small, quiet restaurant, not fancy. I put him down on the seat beside me and dropped the work boots beside him. The waitress came over, saw him through the mesh, but didn't seem to mind. I think she liked us.

"First day on the job?"

"Yah. How did you know?"

"The boots. Tomorrow you'll be wearing them."

"Oh. Yah, you're right. Do you have any spaghetti?"

"All kinds. And the mutt?"

"He likes spaghetti too."

She laughed. "I don't know if it's good for dogs to eat people food."

"It's a special occasion."

Hollie *loved* spaghetti.

"Well, in that case. And to drink?"

"Milk."

"And the special occasion mutt?"

"Water."

"Okee-dokee."

While we waited for our spaghetti to come, I watched a man enter the restaurant, take off his baseball cap, lift a newspaper from the counter and take a seat. The waitress came over and poured him a cup of coffee without saying a word. He was a regular. As I stared at him I felt strange inside. Was he my father? He could have been. He looked a bit like me, only older. What would Ziegfried say? The odds of meeting my father by accident were too low to even consider. And Sheba? There are no accidents; trust your feelings.

The waitress returned to the man. "*Ça va, Pierre?*"

"*Bien.*"

It wasn't my father. Ziegfried would have won that round.

With bellies full of spaghetti we hit the pavement once more. Now I was tired. It had been a lot of walking, a lot of sharpening and a lot of excitement for one day. A full belly always made me feel sleepy. Hollie was already asleep. But I couldn't return to the sub yet. I had to wait until dark and sneak across the empty pier.

When darkness came I was lying behind some bushes next to the train tracks in front of the pier. I had already fallen asleep. Hollie was out of the bag and sleeping with his head on my lap. I put him back in the bag, crossed the tracks and went quietly across the open lot. Halfway across, I saw the lights of a truck.

"Shoot!"

I bent down slowly and froze, kneeling close to the ground, making myself as small as possible. It was a dark night; maybe the truck wouldn't see us.

They didn't. They drove around the circumference of the area and headed back. A routine check. I needed to find a better place to hide the sub. Not tonight though. I was too tired tonight.

Seaweed was on the hatch. He was glad to see us. I didn't know what the food was like for him in Montreal, but he sure was happy to have dog biscuits. He followed us inside.

"Hi, Seaweed. You can hang out with Hollie; I'm going to sleep."

I shut the hatch, went down ten feet, dimmed the lights, climbed onto my cot and fell asleep. The last thing I heard was Seaweed tapping his beak on the rim of the observation window, which was his way of telling Hollie to pass the ball. Like *that* was going to happen.

Second day on the job was fun. Jacob turned out to be a really nice old man. He had a deep love of animals too, and that put him in good stead with Hollie, who also liked that the old man could pull nibbles of food from his pocket every time he came over to visit, which was often.

I was halfway through the saws when the boss came in the room with a wooden box of chisels and dropped it on the floor with a bang. "When you finish the saws!"

He spoke really loudly. That's what happens when you work in a noisy shop all day. Then he went out. Jacob came in next. He bent down, picked up a chisel and ran his thumb along its edge. "There's a couple days' work here."

"I like sharpening."

"You're good at it too. Where'd you learn to sharpen like that?"

"In Newfoundland."

"Uh huh? Somebody was a good teacher."

"Yup."

I never told anyone about Ziegfried or Sheba.

"Any luck finding that Pynsent fella yet?"

"Not yet."

Jacob reached down and fed Hollie a piece of cookie through the open top of the tool bag. Hollie licked his fingers to say thank you.

"I guess you've travelled a long way to look for this fella."

"I suppose."

Jacob could read my mind. I could just tell.

"Hmmm. I did that once. The very same thing, I think."

"Really?"

"Yup. A long time ago. I suppose I was about your age."

"Was it worth it?"

He reached in and patted Hollie's head affectionately.

"No. Not really. How long has this fella been working on the dockyards?"

"Sixteen years."

"You could check out the machine shops by the *Aeolus*."

"What's that?"

"A ship. She's being refitted. If he's been working here that long, there's a good chance you'll find him over there."

Aeolus. Cool name for an ocean freighter. Aeolus was the Greek god of the wind. Sheba talked about Greek gods and goddesses as if they really existed, but surely she didn't believe that? You can't believe in *everything.* That doesn't make sense. Imagine a world where gods, goddesses, ghosts, mermaids, angels and sea monsters were all real. You might as well add fairies, trolls and witches too. What about dragons? Marie believed in the Loch Ness monster. I guess she now believes in the curse of the mummy too. Oh boy!

Chapter 22

AFTER WORK I WALKED up to get paid, bought a sandwich and ate it on the way to search for the *Aeolus*. This time we caught a bus for part of the way back to the dockyards. It was late evening when we found the yard where the *Aeolus* was lying. I was wearing my own pass now that said that I worked at the dockyards, and so I was allowed through the gate. How strange to enter that way instead of sneaking in through the shadows. It was funny how one piece of paper could make so much difference.

The *Aeolus* lay in dry dock like a tired warrior. I didn't like seeing ships out of water. There was something sad about it. Freighters like her sailed all over the world, even up rivers, in all weather. They braved the fiercest storms and kept going even when their decks were caked with ice. They became floating islands for flocks of migrating seabirds that flew thousands of miles every year. Nobody will ever know how many seabirds die every year because they get caught in storms or fall out of the sky from exhaustion. From the air, those birds can spot a freighter for about a thirty mile radius. Finding one must sometimes make the difference between life and death. For me, the freighters, like the seabirds, were noble creatures. I always found it sad to see one pulled out of the water like a dead whale, its rust and barnacles exposed for everyone to see.

But refitting was necessary. There certainly was no shame in tuning up an engine. Ziegfried taught me the importance of that. Why should it be sad to tune up a ship? It was the same thing, and yet it bothered me to see her hauled out of the river.

There was no one around except a few security guards. The machine shop closest to the ship was closed. At least I knew where these shops were now, another place where my father might be working. I quickly scanned the waterfront for places to hide the sub, but didn't see any obvious ones. I would come back on Saturday, when I was off work, and look more closely. And I would come in the sub.

Once I knew where my father worked, all I had to do was go there first thing in the morning, say hello, return to the sub, get back into the river and sail back to Sheba's island.

Then we could prepare for the Pacific. I wouldn't have to return to the shop and sharpen any more tools. Nobody would even remember me after a day or so. Nobody even knew who I really was. And yet . . . that didn't feel right. I thought about it all the way back to the sub.

I couldn't figure it out. Why would it bother me to leave like that? Did I want to become a machinist, like my father? No way! Did I want to live in a little room in the back of an industrial shop, like Jacob did? No. Did I want to live in the city? Not a chance. Then why would I be so reluctant to leave, once I was able?

For the last part of the walk back, Seaweed joined us. He drifted down from the sky like a snowflake, landed beside us and did his little cakewalk of hopping, skipping and fly-ing short spaces to keep up, a little like a vulture. He looked happy and free, so wonderfully free. That's how I wanted to stay, happy and free. No, I didn't belong in the city and I didn't belong in a machine shop. So why would I find it dif-ficult to leave? I told myself I would have the answer by the time I touched the metal of the hatch.

I did. It was my promise. Nothing more than that. By accepting the job I had agreed that I would finish sharpen-ing all of the saws and all of the chisels and blades in the shop. I hadn't promised anything more than that, but I had promised that. It would only take me a few more days. May-be by Saturday. Then I could leave. That is, once I had found my father.

Seaweed came to work with us the next day. He must have had enough of the big city already and decided he didn't belong there either. I could understand. I never thought that anyone would pay attention to another seagull on the dockyards and so I never worried about us being spotted walking along together. But we were.

When we reached the shop, Seaweed flew up to the roof. Hollie and I went inside. As soon as we settled in the tool room and I picked up a chisel, Jacob came in. He was excited. His voice was in a whisper.

"Alfred! I saw you through my window."

"Oh. Yah?"

"You were walking with a seagull!"

"I was?"

"Yes. You were. Alfred. I have something to show you. Come down to my room for a second."

"Umm . . . okay, just for a second. I'm just getting started."

"It will only take a second. I promise."

I picked up the tool bag and followed Jacob down the hall. Hollie wouldn't appreciate being left behind. Jacob's room was just another large closet at the very end of the hallway, but it had a larger window, a fridge, hotplate, TV, sleeping cot and small bookshelf. It was kind of cozy. He pulled out a seat for me. I sat down with Hollie on my lap. Jacob reached for something under his bed. It was a scrapbook, big and fat and stuffed with newspaper clippings. He opened it delicately and turned its pages with care. I caught a glimpse of photos of ships and submarines, old ones and new ones. Why did he have pictures of submarines? What was this adding up to? He found the page he was looking for, stared at it closely for a minute and grinned.

"There! Hah!"

He turned the book around and brought it over and pointed to a newspaper clipping from the Montreal *Gazette.* It was a photo of me handing a family over to the coastguard. I had rescued them from their capsized sailboat in a storm. Seaweed was standing on the hatch behind me. The caption read: "*Submarine Outlaw Assists Coastguard with Rescue.*"

"That's you!" said Jacob excitedly.

I looked him in the eye, took a breath, paused, then let it out. "Yah."

"I knew it! You're the Submarine Outlaw!"

"Could you please not tell anyone?"

He put his hand over his heart. "My word."

I flipped through the pages of the scrapbook very carefully. It was filled with cut-outs from newspapers, some of them old and faded. There were pictures of ship launches, sinkings, wrecks and piracy. There were oil-spills, drilling rigs, explosions and accidents. I saw the *Carolus*, the Newfoundland ferry, and the U-boat that sank her. There were pictures of the building of the St. Lawrence Seaway. There was the Queen, President Nixon and Pierre Trudeau. I felt honoured to be in the same scrapbook.

"Wow, you have kept this book for a long time."

"Yup. I have. I never thought I'd meet somebody who was *in* it."

"So, were you a sailor?"

"No. Wanted to be though."

"How come you didn't?"

He shrugged. "Ahhhh, that's life, isn't it? You spend your life dreaming of doing certain things while you're busy doing other things."

"Not me. I'm living the life that I want. That's why I went to sea in my submarine. I'm an explorer."

"You are indeed, Alfred. You are indeed."

He closed his book and looked at me. "But why did you come to Montreal?"

"Oh. Well, this is actually the first time I did something I didn't want to do. I'm looking for my father. A friend of mine told me it was a good idea. She said I would live with unfinished business for the rest of my life if I didn't."

Jacob frowned. "We always live with unfinished business, Alfred. I've never known anybody who didn't."

"Really?"

"Yup."

"Oh."

He was wearing a strange expression on his face. I had the feeling he was leading up to something. He was.

"Can I ask you something?"

"Sure."

"It's a strange request."

"Okay?"

"Would you give an old man a ride in your submarine?"

Oh boy. How could I answer that? I hated to disappoint anyone, especially someone as nice as Jacob. But I had promised myself that I wouldn't take passengers in the sub any more, except in the case of emergencies. And I had meant it. As I stared into his kind face I asked myself if a promise to myself was just as important as a promise to somebody else.

At first I thought that it wasn't, I really did. But when I opened my mouth to answer him, the words wouldn't come out. Something inside me told me it was the same. If I couldn't keep a promise to myself, why would I keep a promise to anybody else? Besides, the danger was real. I had learned that with Marie. What if Jacob panicked and got injured while riding in the sub? Was I willing to take responsibility for that?

I looked him in the eye when I answered. "I'm really very sorry. I promised myself I wouldn't take passengers any more because it is dangerous and I don't feel able to protect them well enough. I'm sorry."

I saw disappointment cloud his eyes and his smile drop. He nodded his head with resignation. "I understand. You're a conscientious young man, Alfred."

Did he really understand? I hoped he did but couldn't tell. I knew I had done the right thing though. I knew it, even though it didn't feel good.

Early Saturday morning I took the sub upriver until I spotted the *Aeolus*. She wasn't easy to see from the water. There were buildings in the way and another ship docked nearby. Through the periscope I scanned the pier. Outside of the shop closest to the *Aeolus* I saw half a dozen men gather. It was too far to see them clearly but one of the men did something that startled me. He danced a little jig. Probably it was nothing more than a coincidence but my grandmother once told me that my father was fond of dancing the jig. Could that man on the pier be my father?

Chapter 23

BY THE END OF the day on Saturday I had mostly finished sharpening the tools. There were a few left but it was questionable whether they were worth saving. I felt I could leave in good conscience.

Sunday we stayed in the sub, listened to music, cleaned up and rested. We needed the rest. I considered moving the sub to another spot where it would be better hidden, but that would have taken all day and I figured we'd only be around a day or two more at the most, so we stayed put.

On Monday we were on our way through the streets of the city in the early hours of the morning. Hollie trotted beside me. Seaweed flew above us. We went down to the dockyard where the *Aeolus* lay. She was a great old ship up close. I was glad she was being refitted.

As we passed the machine shops I felt butterflies in my stomach. No matter how I tried to downplay it I couldn't escape the thought that maybe I was about to meet my father. My grandfather's words echoed in my head. "He's not like you!"

Of course he wasn't like me. Why would he be like me? We weren't the same person.

I saw a group of men collect outside the door of the shop nearest the ship. I was pretty sure it was the same group I had seen on Saturday. My heart started to pound in my chest. Why was I so nervous? I took a deep breath and told myself to calm down. I hadn't come all this way to turn around now.

All of the men were bigger than me—not much taller, but bigger. They were heavier, stronger. They moved with confidence mostly, though I couldn't tell if it were the kind of confidence that ran on the surface or ran deep. And I knew the difference. Ziegfried had the kind of confidence that ran deep. So did Sheba.

There was a young man standing next to an older man and kind of hanging on to him the way a young dog will hang on to an older dog. His name was Bim. I saw it on his jacket. He was a little taller, thicker and older than me. When the older man laughed, he laughed too. But he didn't show any confidence at all. Something about him made me glad I wasn't choosing a life here.

When I walked up to the group, they stopped talking. They stood with cigarettes in their hands and stared at me. The young man jumped right at me. He was unfriendly.

"What do *you* want?"

I didn't answer. I knew he wasn't the one in charge. If I talked to him first, I wouldn't get anywhere. The older men wouldn't respect me if I spoke to him first.

"Can we help you, son?" said an older man. He sounded kind. "Looking for work?"

I nodded and took my time answering. "Yup."

"There's no work here for you," snapped Bim.

I ignored him. I looked at the man beside him, who was staring at me but not saying anything. Was he the man who had danced the jig? Was he my father? I took a deep breath.

"What kind of work are you looking for? Have you got any experience?" said the kind man. His name was Hugh. It was sewn onto his jacket too. The other men weren't wearing their jackets.

"Some. I can sharpen tools, clean engines, cut glass and metal."

"Big deal," said Bim quietly.

"Where did you work last?" said Hugh.

"I'm working on the east dock."

"You're working now?"

"Yes."

"Then why did you come down here?"

"I finished sharpening all the tools over there. Now I'm sitting around waiting for them to get dull."

Everyone laughed except Bim. The man beside him threw his cigarette butt to the ground and stepped on it. "Where are you from?"

"Newfoundland."

"I figured. Where in Newfoundland?"

"The north shore."

"The north shore where?"

"All over, kind of."

"Oh yah? What's your name?"

"Peddle."

His eyes opened wide. "Is that right? Lots of Peddles in Newfoundland."

"Yup."

"There's no work for you here," repeated Bim.

The man beside him opened his mouth again. "I don't think . . ."

"We've got some saws and chisels that could use a sharpening," said Hugh. "Come in and show us what you can do."

"Hey! . . . I sharpened those already," said Bim defensively.

Hugh looked as if he had forgotten that. "Oh. Yah. Well, they can always use a little more attention. A saw can never be too sharp."

Hugh winked at me. Bim made an ugly face. "I already sharpened those," he said under his breath.

Why was he so unfriendly? Was he afraid I would take his job? I wouldn't. I wasn't planning on staying around long enough to take anyone's job. Anyway, that was his problem, not mine.

I followed Hugh inside to a tool room similar to the one in the other shop, except that this one didn't have a window. Some of the tools were reasonably sharp and some were pretty beaten up. I picked up a saw that looked like a row of broken shark's teeth. Maybe someone had tried to cut concrete with it.

"Some of these are beyond saving. Just do what you can."

Hugh had a tough looking face but it would break into the warmest smile. It made me think that really kind people were a little bit like lighthouses at sea; they showed you a way through the storm. "I'd ahh . . . give young Bim there a wide berth if I were you. He hasn't been here long and he's carrying a whole pack of troubles of his own. Sometimes they send us young fellas from the correctional centre. Sometimes it works out just great and sometimes it don't."

"I understand. Thank you. I will."

I put Hollie down and got to work. It was strange beyond words to know that my father might be in the same building, maybe working at an industrial lathe.

Hugh came back in a few hours to tell me it was time for a break. He picked up two saws I had sharpened, drew his fingers along the points of their teeth, pulled his glasses from his pocket, put them on and looked down the rows of teeth from base to tip. He nodded with approval. "Yup. You know what you're doing. Good workers from Newfoundland."

He looked at me and lowered his voice. "You look like Buddy."

He pointed with his face in the direction of the room where the industrial lathes were. "Are you related?"

Was Buddy the man who had danced the jig and asked me about Newfoundland? I didn't think he looked like me.

"I don't think so."

"You don't *think* so?"

"No."

"But you don't *know* so?"

Hugh reminded me of Sheba in a way. He seemed to understand things without needing them explained, and was kind.

"No. I guess not."

"I see. Does he know?"

"I don't know."

"Planning on asking him?"

"Maybe. I'm not sure. I'm not planning on staying around."

"Oh. I see. You just want to find somebody, then fly."

"More or less."

"I understand."

I felt that he really did.

"Maybe Buddy knows already. But don't count on him coming out and telling you."

"I won't."

"All the way from Newfoundland, eh? How did you get here, hitchhike?"

"*Something* like that."

I wanted to be honest with him but I couldn't tell him about the sub. When I went outside, the men were standing around smoking. Smoking was strictly forbidden around industrial equipment, so the men would smoke outside. Buddy wasn't there now. Bim came right over to me. He couldn't get his words out quickly enough. "Do you speak French?"

"No."

"Then what are you doing in Quebec?"

I didn't answer right away. I couldn't figure out what his problem was.

"I'm not planning on staying in Quebec."

"That's good."

Suddenly Buddy came out. He came right over to Bim and he looked angry. "Did you shut off the press?"

"Yah. Of course I did."

"No you didn't."

"I did! I know I did."

"Then how come it's still running?"

"I dunno, but I turned it off. I know I did."

Buddy shook his head angrily. He didn't believe him. He looked at Bim as if he were worthless. I felt sorry for him. Buddy's accusation took the spirit out of him like a hole in a balloon.

When I was finished for the day, I went out the door closest to Buddy's work area. He frowned when he saw me coming. I didn't know if he was my father. I didn't know if he knew either. Probably not. I almost didn't care because he wasn't very nice. If he didn't feel like talking, then, neither did I.

"Peddle!"

"Yah?"

"You can cut glass?"

"Yes."

"Where'd you learn to do that?"

"In a shop."

"In Newfoundland?"

"Yes."

"That's a useful skill."

He reached into his shirt pocket for a pack of cigarettes and went towards the door. I followed him out.

"Where was the shop?"

"Uhh . . . outside of Grand Falls."

"Grand Falls?"

That wasn't exactly true but it was close enough. "Yah."

I wished he would stop asking me questions. Suddenly Seaweed dropped out of the sky, landed on the edge of the pier and squawked at me. He wanted a snack. Buddy reached down, picked up a stone and threw it at him. The stone missed by a foot and Seaweed flew away.

"Don't!" I shouted.

"What's your problem? It's just a seagull. They're a nuisance."

"I like them. They're smart."

He rolled his eyes at me, then looked more closely. "What tools are you carrying on your back anyway? I've never seen you take that bag off."

"I'm not carrying tools in it."

Now he was curious. "So, what's in the bag?"

"My dog."

"You're kidding, right?"

I shook my head.

"Lemme see."

I pulled the bag around to my front and opened it. He looked inside. Hollie stared up at him, wagging his tail. Buddy burst out laughing. "That's not a dog, that's a rat! Why don't you get yourself a real dog?"

I shut the bag and swung it around my back.

"Ah, don't be like that. Can't you take a joke?"

Not from you, I thought. "I've got to go."

"Oh, come on. Don't be like that. Come out and have a beer with us. Be a man!"

"Maybe another time."

I turned to leave.

"Okay, Peddle. But remember: the dockyard's a place for real men, not animal lovers."

Yah, well, real men don't throw stones at seagulls, I thought, but didn't say it out loud.

I wished I had.

As I turned the corner, went down the long side of the building and crossed the back alley, Bim was waiting for me.

Chapter 24

"YOU THINK YOU'RE something just because you can sharpen tools, don't you?"

Bim was standing in front of me, blocking my way. He looked like a wild animal. I knew that whatever was making him so angry really had nothing to do with me. But that didn't matter. He had chosen to turn his anger on me and nothing I could say was going to change that. It did occur to me to offer to show him how to sharpen tools properly, and I might have if he wasn't being such a jerk. "What do you want?"

"I don't like you," he said.

I had been taught that a bully is really just a coward. It's fear that drives a bully, fear that turns into anger that he then takes out on somebody else. And if the bully can pass that fear on to somebody else, especially somebody smaller, then he might feel a little better for a while. But it only works if the other person accepts the fear. If he doesn't, the bully has to keep it. That's why it is so important to stand up to a bully. That's what I was taught by my grandfather, and by Ziegfried.

But it wasn't easy.

Bim came right towards me. "I said, I don't like you."

"Why? What did I ever do to you?"

"You're here aren't you?"

"Yah, but I'm not staying. I'm probably leaving tomorrow."

"Yah, well you shouldn't have come in the first place."

I was hoping to remove Bim's excuse for being mad at me. But he was like a wind-up toy that had been wound too far. He needed to let out all that anger and had already made up his mind that it was going to be on me. He jumped forward and pushed me. I fell backwards, lost my balance and fell, but picked myself up quickly. I checked to see that Hollie was okay. He was still riding on my back.

"I don't want to fight you, Bim."

"Well that's too bad then, isn't it?"

I pulled the strap over my head so that I could set the bag down on the ground if I had too. Bim lunged forward really quickly, grabbed the strap out of my hand and threw the bag as far as he could.

"Stop!"

I ran for Hollie, but Bim caught me, grabbed me around the neck and threw me to the ground. He was stronger than me.

"*Stop it!* Why are you doing this? I never did anything to you!"

He was really crazy now. Nothing I said was going to make any difference. I was trying to think of what to do but everything was happening so fast. If I were all by myself, probably I would try to run away. But there was no way I could outrun Bim with Hollie on my back. And there was no way I was leaving without Hollie.

I stood up. I would have to fight him, even though he was bigger and stronger than me. Then he did something that really scared me. He picked up a board, a broken and jagged two-by-four. A fist fight was one thing. You might get some bruises and a black eye, but getting hit by a board could cause a serious injury.

Now I felt desperate to protect myself. I rushed to the pile of debris closest to me. My hand fell on a long thin piece of pipe. It was gas pipe, about three quarters of an inch thick. When I pulled it free, it was about seven feet long.

It was never my intention to strike Bim with the pipe, only to defend myself. But he rushed at me, yelling at the top of his lungs, and he swung the board at me. It happened so fast, all I could do was duck. And then, I swung the pipe around in an arc, as hard as I could, but I aimed it low, close to the ground. I never wanted to hit him on the head. I never wanted to hurt him, only to defend myself. The pipe caught him on his shins, and he went down. And he cried.

He coiled up in a ball with his hands around his shins and he bawled like a baby. It must have been really painful. I dropped the pipe and ran over to Hollie. I opened up the bag and ran my hand over his head. "Are you okay, Hollie?"

He barked excitedly. He was happy to see me. I picked up the tool bag, put it around my shoulder and was about to hurry away. I looked at Bim. He was still curled up on the ground holding his shins and crying. I came a little closer. I really felt sorry for him.

"Are you going to be okay?"

He didn't answer.

"Do you think it's broken?"

No answer.

"I didn't want to fight you, you know."

He was still crying, though I couldn't tell how much was for the pain and how much for something else. I had a feeling there was something else.

"Well, I hope it's not broken."

I turned and left. Before we went out of sight I looked back one last time. Bim was still sitting on the ground but had raised his head and was staring at the river. I wondered what he was thinking.

On our way back, I let Hollie walk. Seaweed joined us. I could tell they were ready to leave. I wanted to so much too, but couldn't. Not yet. Just one more day, I told myself. I hadn't told Buddy who I was. He hadn't told me. It wouldn't feel right to leave yet. Everything felt more unfinished now than before we had come.

We walked up to our favourite restaurant for a double serving of spaghetti, apple pie and ice cream. Debbie, the waitress, greeted us with a big smile. "Spaghetti, Al?"

"Yes, please."

"And how is 'Special-occasion' mutt today?" she said sweetly, and reached inside the tool bag and scratched Hollie's face. Hollie loved Debbie because she was the one who brought us spaghetti.

"He's had a tough day today."

"Has he?"

She clicked her tongue, blew him a kiss and went to serve other customers. We sat at our regular booth and looked around and tried not to feel impatient. We were hungry. We were regulars now. That was a pleasant feeling. I put my feet up and patted Hollie's fur. Seaweed was probably on the roof. I would save him a piece of garlic bread.

My head was spinning. I surely never expected to be in a fight. The dockyards was a rough place, I guessed. Good thing Hollie was okay. Bim had lots of problems, that was for sure. Maybe he came from a broken home. It was too bad Buddy wasn't nicer to him. That would help. If Bim had a chance to work with somebody like Ziegfried for a while it would do him a world of good. Ziegfried would treat him with respect, because Ziegfried treated everyone with respect. That was his nature. Buddy treated Bim with contempt. What chance did he have with that?

It really didn't feel like Buddy was my father. Hugh said that he looked like me but I didn't think so. I couldn't feel it. What would Sheba have said about that? Buddy was definitely from Newfoundland. But so what? Lots of people were from Newfoundland. And in Newfoundland, everyone called everyone else Buddy. Was Buddy's real name Russell?

If he *was* my father, I didn't like him. I knew that much already. We didn't have anything in common. I didn't see how I could ever like someone who didn't like animals, especially somebody who threw stones at them. Sheba said it didn't matter if I liked him or not, all I had to do was meet him face to face and tell him who I was. Okay, I would, tomorrow. Tomorrow I would confront Buddy, tell him who I was and find out if he was my father. I'd get it over with. Then, we could return to the river, sail back to Newfoundland, prepare for the Pacific and do what I was put on this earth to do: explore.

With full bellies we crossed the long pier in the dark. I waited until the security truck made its rounds, then started off across the open space. The moon was out. A couple of times I felt that someone was following us. I didn't see anyone, just shadows, but the shadows were moving and the feeling was strong. Hollie kept turning around too. He stared and sniffed. We looked at each other.

"What is it, Hollie?"

He sensed something. We both did. But there was no one there. We climbed into the sub, the three of us, and I turned the lights low.

As I lay down on my cot and drifted off to sleep, I suddenly remembered it was my birthday. I was sixteen now. Cool.

Bim didn't show up for work the next morning. I wasn't surprised. Probably his leg was too sore to stand on all day.

I went back to sharpening saws, chisels and the blades of a few axes and hatchets. These were very secondary tools in a machine shop set up for refitting a ship and they tended to get used for things other than their original purpose. The axes, for instance, had been driven into something much harder than wood, so that their blades were flattened out like putty on a knife. I had to run them through an industrial grinder for quite a while before I could take a sharpening stone to them. The chisels looked as if they were being used to puncture holes in steel. Maybe they were. Probably it was cheaper just to buy new chisels than pay a full-time worker to sit and sharpen the old ones, which is why they piled up in a box.

About mid-morning, Hugh stuck his head through the door. "Break!"

I picked up Hollie and went out. Nobody bothered me about having a dog at work because I kept him in the bag and he was as quiet as a mouse. Neither Hollie nor I liked being around the cigarette smoke outside but we had to accept it. It would have been unthinkable not to stand with the other men during break. Buddy came out last and he was in a bad mood. I could tell from the way the other men stepped carefully around him. He wasn't bigger than any of them but he was more intense. Today, he completely ignored me, as if I wasn't even there. Well, I was going to confront him anyway. And then, something completely unexpected happened. A man stepped outside and yelled: "Russell! It's your daughter on the phone."

I stared at Buddy. Now I knew it was him. How many Russells from Newfoundland were working on the dockyards of Montreal? Even Ziegfried would find that a bit of a coincidence. And yet Buddy didn't react. Hadn't he heard?

"Russell! The phone!"

"Tell her I'm busy! I can't come to the phone."

The voice had come from behind me. I turned. There was another man standing there all by himself. I didn't know why I hadn't noticed him before. Maybe he hadn't been there. He was not very big. He didn't look or sound much like the others. He seemed reserved and quiet, rather shy. The other men seemed to ignore him. He didn't look like me either, I thought, and yet, something about him was strangely familiar. What was it? Was it his voice? Was it his movements? I couldn't tell what it was but I could feel it. I felt tingles in my spine. Was this my father?

"Take the call, Russell, that's the third time she's called this month already."

"Tell her . . . ah, yah, okay!"

He stamped out his cigarette and went inside. I was stunned. I looked at Hugh. He must have read my face.

"Oh . . . yah. That's Russell. That's his girl from his first wife, umm . . . or his second, I guess. I dunno. He doesn't live with her anymore. He lives somewhere else now."

I was so shocked I didn't know what to think. "Do . . . do you know how old she is?"

"Who? His daughter? Ahhhh . . . no. She's younger than you, I think. I'm not sure. He doesn't see her too much. As you can tell."

"Why?"

Hugh shrugged his shoulders. "I dunno."

Russell came back out. He went past me without looking at me. He kept to himself. Suddenly, Buddy spoke up. "So . . . Peddle. I see you're still here. You didn't run back to New-foundland yet?"

I shook my head then turned to see if Russell had heard that. He was staring straight at me now in a confused way. Yes. He had heard. The name "Peddle" meant something him. He looked like he was wrestling with it. The men started in. I followed. As I passed the phone stand I noticed a binder labelled *Contact Info*. I wanted to look at it but didn't want anyone to see me. Russell had a daughter. If he was my father that meant that I had a sister. I couldn't believe it. But as I returned to the tool room and sat down, all I could think of was getting my hands on that binder.

It was hard to concentrate. I picked up a chisel and the sharpening stone. The chisel had gouges cut into its edge. It was useless as a chisel like that. In fact, it would destroy anything it was properly applied to. But you could certainly puncture holes with it, if you hit it hard enough. But why not use a proper tool for that, like a punch? This chisel would have to run through the grinder. I dropped it into the box and picked up another one. It had tiny nicks but I could remove them with the coarse side of the stone. I turned and looked at Hollie. He was staring at me through the mesh of the tool bag.

"We should go."

He wagged his tail.

"I'll be right back."

I jumped up and went to the phone stand. I took the receiver and put it to my ear, then pressed some buttons to make it look like I was making a call. The receiver started beeping but I ignored it. I pulled the contact book down, opened it and flipped through it quickly. Under "P" I found "Pynsent, Russell." That pretty much confirmed it. I had found my father. I took a deep breath and tried to calm down. I needed to think straight.

There were several addresses and phone numbers, all crossed out with heavy pencil except the last one. The one at the top of the page read: "Antoinette Babbette, 269, rue de la Rivière Ouest, Dorval." None of the other addresses included a name other than Russell's. I scribbled down Antoinette's address on a piece of paper, shut the book, put it back and hung up the phone. As I turned, I saw Russell standing there watching me. I turned red. I folded the piece of paper and put it in my pocket. When I looked up again, he was gone.

I went back to the tool room and sat down. Hugh came in. His face was soft and compassionate. "So. You figure it's Russell?"

I nodded. "Looks like it."

He shook his head. "Don't expect to get much out of him. I haven't heard him put more than two sentences together in all the time I've known him. He's a good worker though."

I stared at the chisel box and thought about it. "All the same, I'm going to talk to him today."

"You can't."

I raised my head. "Why not?"

"Because he's gone home."

I stayed and finished the day. Because my father hadn't, I wanted to. I didn't know why. I hated quitting. I hated the very thought of it. Besides, I wanted to think, and sharpening tools was the kind of work that helped me do that.

But as the hours passed, the only things that got sharper were the tools. My mind just went around in circles. I had never expected my father to run away from me. It shouldn't have surprised me I supposed, when I thought about it. Still, I wondered what he was so afraid of.

When we left for the day, I shook hands with Hugh, thanked him for the job and apologized for not staying longer. He stood at the door. "No worries. Just remember something, will you?"

"Sure. What is it?"

He looked me in the eye. I found it difficult to look back because I was upset. "Nobody's perfect. Russell's a decent man."

I nodded, shook his hand and left. But his words stayed with me.

Chapter 25

WE HAD BEEN FOLLOWED. I was certain of it. Someone kept creating shadows and the shadows kept moving. Hollie was always looking back. But we never saw anyone. Weird. Could it have been a ghost? I didn't see any light. If ghosts were really what Sheba said they were it was unlikely one would follow us. But the feeling was strong.

We crossed the long pier. Clouds drifted across the city and covered the moon, although the city was never dark at night in the way the river was. There were too many lights everywhere to allow for much darkness, even on the dockyards. We climbed into the sub. I fed the crew, dimmed the lights and got ready for bed.

My submarine was my sanctuary. That's what Sheba had called it. She said your sanctuary was the place you felt happiest, where you could sit and think and work out things that were bothering you. It was where you felt safest. I would have thought Sheba's sanctuary was her kitchen but she said it was her bedroom. That's where she practised yoga. That's where she read. Well, my sub certainly was mine. I think it was Hollie's sanctuary too. I couldn't speak for Seaweed. He was happy almost anywhere, except that whenever he settled down by the observation window in the middle of a storm, I bet it felt like a sanctuary to him. It was our home. Sheba said Ziegfried's sanctuary was his workshop.

But when I lay down I couldn't sleep. My mind kept racing. Half an hour later I jumped up, dressed, told the crew I'd be right back, and went out. There was something I needed to do. In my pocket I carried the paper with Antoinette Babbette's phone number. Maybe it was not too late to call.

I went quickly across the long yard. The patrol truck was not in sight. There was a phone booth on the other side of the train tracks, but I had to go around the gate. By myself I could climb along the seawall. Just as I reached the end of the yard, where the grain elevators rose in the dark, I turned and looked back. For a second, I thought I saw a shadow move in the centre, the very spot where I had knelt down to hide from the truck. It must have been my imagination. What were the chances that somebody else was doing exactly what I had done?

I started to go, then stopped. Wasn't that exactly why it had worked for me when I had hidden from the truck, because no one expected a shadow to turn into a person? I decided to take a minute and stare at that spot. If nothing moved in one minute I would continue. I waited. It was difficult to see across in the dark. It was probably nothing. But then, I thought I saw something move. Sure enough, the shadow shivered and shook. A few seconds later it stood up. It wasn't a ghost. It was Bim!

I waited for a few seconds to see what he would do. He started off in the direction of the sub. Yikes! I went after him, walking briskly, hoping he wouldn't see me. But he did, and he started to run. No! I broke into my fastest run. I had to catch him before he found the sub.

He wasn't running very fast because of his leg but he had too much of a head start for me to catch him. By the time I reached the centre, he was near the end of the yard, where the wall was. I watched him go over it. He had found the sub.

I ran so hard my lungs burned and my legs ached. I had to catch him before he climbed inside. Hollie and Seaweed were inside. What if he opened the hatch and flooded it? What if he climbed in and threw some switches? Any number of things could happen. All of them were bad.

I was too late. When I scrambled over the wall, all I saw were bubbles. Bubbles were coming up where the sub had been moored but they weren't moving forward, which told me that, so far, the sub had only gone straight down. Bim couldn't start the engine unless he was on the surface, but he probably didn't know that. He likely flipped the dive switch because it was the first one on the panel board. The sub would hit bottom pretty hard unless he pumped air into the tanks first, which I doubted he would.

My mind raced through the possibilities. The river was sixty feet deep at this spot. The sub would strike bottom hard but probably not hard enough to suffer damage, unless there was a sharp object jutting up from the bottom that might strike the observation window. It was unlikely anything would puncture the glass because it was so thick, but a sharp blow might jar it loose, causing a leak. The greater danger was that sooner or later Bim would figure out how to engage the batteries and put the sub in gear. Then he'd be on the move. He would enter the river, not be able to steer, nor judge his depth and would strike something—a pier, a riverbank, another vessel. There was a good chance the sub would get damaged or destroyed and he, Hollie and Seaweed killed.

How could I have let this happen? Why hadn't I moved the sub to a safer location? I felt sick to my stomach as I took a deep breath and jumped into the river.

The sub had gone straight down. I figured it would come straight back up before he did anything else. The simplest thing to do in the sub was to go up and down because those two switches were right in front of you on the panel board.

They just released a steady stream of air, or water, into the tanks unless you adjusted the valves manually, which he wouldn't know how to do. So, I expected him to go down and come right back up, picking up speed in both directions as he went. On the other hand, if the sub were sitting on the bottom, I had to dive only fifty feet to reach it. But I couldn't see, and might run into it on its way up.

I went down as carefully as possible, with my hands in front of my face. At about twenty feet the hull of the sub hit me hard and knocked me out of the way. I tried desperately to reach a handle on the portal but never had a chance. Within seconds I heard the sub surface above me. I went after it, but before I could break the surface and grab a breath of air, it had started down again. I had to let it go. I couldn't follow it down without more air in my lungs.

I had no idea if Bim was having a good time or not. Maybe he was terrified. I grabbed a breath of air and went down again. I couldn't wait for him to surface; he might figure out the controls and sail away.

The sub was sitting on the bottom when I reached it this time. As soon as I took hold of a handle we started to rise. We started slowly but would pick up speed, and, unless he let water into the tanks, we would break the surface dramatically.

That's exactly what happened. I found it painful in my chest coming up because I didn't have enough air. I was far from relaxed and never had a chance to breathe properly before diving. My lungs were bursting when we rose out of the river like a whale snorting. Likely we were drawing attention from someone somewhere but there wasn't anything I could do about that. I grabbed as much air as I could this time because I figured we would go right back down again. And we did.

The best thing would be if I could open the hatch on the surface, jump inside and shut it before we submerged again. Then, I would have to deal with Bim. I wasn't looking forward to that. But there was another possibility. I could open the hatch underwater, climb in and shut it.

The sub would flood if I did that of course. But Ziegfried had designed the sub to deal with just such an emergency. And we had tested it. Even with the hatch closing immediately, the river would rush in and fill the sub at least half full and it would plunge to the bottom. After fifteen minutes or so the sump pumps would remove enough water to make the sub buoyant again. But it was extremely frightening to be inside when this was happening.

I held on to the handle with two hands as the sub pulled me under. We went down quickly and I knew we were going to hit hard. I placed my feet against the hull and bent my knees to absorb the blow. I didn't want to lose my grip. Someone else was in my sub with my crew. This was never supposed to happen.

We hit with a crashing sound, which was probably some kind of debris on the bottom. I hoped that's what it was.

Within seconds we were rising again. He was flipping the same two switches. Was he having fun or was he panicking? Was he trying to destroy my submarine? Surely he didn't want to drown?

On the way up I tried to prepare for opening the hatch. If he kept doing what he had been doing, I would have maybe ten seconds to open the hatch, climb in and shut it. That was enough time if I were ready. But halfway up I heard the sound that I didn't want to hear—the whir of the propeller. He had engaged the batteries and put the sub in gear. We were staring to move. We were no longer rising.

This was the toughest decision I ever had to make. What should I do: open the hatch and bring the river inside the sub, fight with Bim and rescue my crew; or, let go and let him ride the sub until he crashed it, for surely he would crash? There was no time to think it over. If I had had more time, would I have chosen differently? Maybe. Maybe not. I would never know. With half a minute of air left in my lungs at most, I spun the wheel on the hatch and pulled it open.

Chapter 26

≈

I HEARD SCREAMING inside as water flooded the sub. If Bim had been having fun, he wasn't anymore. My first concern was for Hollie and Seaweed, although both were excellent swimmers and the sub was their home. They had often seen water rush in through the portal, though never like this. I was more afraid that he might injure them in his panic, and I knew he was going to panic.

I had barely pulled the hatch shut when Bim came scrambling up the ladder beneath me. Everything was happening so fast but I could tell that he was panicking. The flooding water had risen to his chest and was knocking him around. I had to kick him off the ladder to prevent him from interfering with sealing the hatch. I kicked him down, he scrambled up and I kicked him down again. We were sinking fast. Any moment we would strike bottom. He was wailing his head off like someone who had stepped into a hornets' nest.

He was just starting for the ladder again when the sub hit. I lost my grip and fell on top of him. I knocked him right under the water, though I didn't mean to. He was still panicking, even though no more water was coming inside, and the sump pumps were pumping out the water that had come in. He couldn't know that. Once a person starts to panic, it takes a long time for them to settle down.

He raised his head above water and I realized he was choking. He had swallowed water. Like a crazy person he pushed past me and went for the ladder again. This time I held on to his legs to keep him from reaching the hatch. He didn't even seem to understand that we were on the bottom of the river. He just wanted to get out.

"It's okay!" I yelled. "It's okay now!"

He didn't hear me. I pulled on his leg with all my weight. I had to keep him from reaching the hatch. Bending my head, I peeked into the bow and saw Seaweed floating around, and beside him, Hollie, his little head just above water as he swam around in circles. I realized now that Bim had not been having a good time in the sub at all. He had probably been panicking even before I came in. Maybe he couldn't swim.

"Calm down!" I yelled. "It's going to be okay!"

He couldn't hear me and I was getting tired trying to hold him. I had to think of something else. I let go of him for a second and he rushed up to the hatch. I rushed up beside him. Then, by pushing back against him in the tight space, I was able to pin him against the ladder. He couldn't move his arms freely enough to open the hatch. Now, it was just a matter of time. When the sump pumps removed enough water to make the sub buoyant again, it would lift off the bottom and surface automatically. That was how Ziegfried had designed it, and I had perfect confidence in Ziegfried.

But it seemed to take forever. And it was exhausting pinning Bim against the ladder. In the fright of his panic he started to cry. When he couldn't move, his crying gradually turned into weeping. It was very sad and I felt sorry for him. At the same time, I couldn't let him go.

"It's going to be okay," I said. "I promise you."

After what felt like hours, but was probably less than ten minutes, the sub gently lifted off the river floor. It was heavy still. The rising would be slow. When we broke the surface, I would have to act quickly. I had no idea what was waiting for us up there.

I knew when we surfaced because the sub bobbed from side to side. It had picked up speed on the way up, with water being pumped out all the way. I let Bim open the hatch, which he did with desperation, and climb out into the darkness. But there were lights, and there were voices.

It was the river police. They were coming over quickly. I

heard a voice over a megaphone. First it came in French; then in English.

"This is the police! Surrender your vessel! I repeat! This is the police! Surrender your vessel!"

I still didn't know if Bim could swim or not. Two police boats were drawing near.

"Bim! Can you swim?"

He looked at me pathetically.

"Do you know how to swim?" I asked.

He didn't answer. He was frightened to death. I grabbed a lifebuoy as quickly as I could. "Here! Put this on!"

I raised his arms and pulled it down over him. He was too frightened to resist.

"Hold on here!" I said, and took hold of his wrists and pulled his hands over to a handle on the side of the portal. He grabbed hold. I knew he wouldn't let go. The boats were almost upon us anyway.

"Surrender your vessel, NOW!" yelled the man with the megaphone.

If I surrendered I would be arrested. They would take the sub for sure. They would take Hollie and Seaweed too. Our sailing days would be over. I would never get the sub back.

If Bim's life had been in danger, I would have acted differently. I would never have left him on the hull that way. But the police were only seconds away. They were going to rescue him.

I climbed back inside and pulled the hatch down, careful not to catch Bim's clothing with it. When I was sure he was clear of the hatch, I sealed it, jumped down and rushed to the controls. The instant I felt them jump onto the hull I hit the dive switch. We started to dive. I raced to the periscope and spun it around to see if they were attaching a cable. No. Two officers were holding on to Bim and helping him to their boat. They were already up to their chests in water. They must have been furious at me.

We went down fifty feet and I checked the crew. Hollie was excited but okay. Seaweed wasn't the least bit disturbed, or didn't show it. Everything was soaking wet, including my bed, but I could dry it all by raising the temperature and taking stuff outside eventually. First, we had to get away from there.

The easiest thing to do was to sail downstream with the current. But that's probably what the police would expect me to do, and so that's what I knew I shouldn't do. Better to do the unpredictable thing if you didn't want to get caught. Did I ever not want to get caught! What would they think of me now, almost drowning somebody and running away from the police? I had refused to surrender my vessel when they had ordered me to. I was definitely a criminal now. They would put me in jail if they caught me, or in a correctional centre, just as Bim had been.

I headed upstream under full battery power with my eyes glued to the sonar screen. I needed to find a good place to hide, a place where no one would find us and we could lie low for a while.

Hollie jumped onto my lap. He was still frightened. I

could see it in his eyes. I stroked his ears and spoke softly to him to calm his excitement. "That was a close one, hey, buddy? I think maybe we need to find better places to hide, don't you?"

I was making so many mistakes. I had made three big mistakes on this voyage: throwing the anchor without thinking, losing the sub in the river and leaving it where someone could find it. The spot I had chosen in Montreal was only safe for a brief mooring, not a whole week, and I knew that when I moored it there. But I had grown comfortable with it and didn't want to bother moving. The truth was the sub was too much temptation, especially for someone like Bim. Would I have opened the hatch and climbed inside if I were him and had discovered it? Yes, I would have. I knew that I would have. And if he had drowned, and Hollie and Seaweed had drowned, would that have been my fault? I shuddered to admit it, but yes, it would have. It was my responsibility to keep the sub hidden from people who might try to take it. And I *was* trying. But sometimes it was so hard.

Nobody's perfect, Hugh had said. True enough, but I couldn't make any more mistakes. I just couldn't. I shut my eyes and promised myself I would be more careful. I promised Hollie and Seaweed too.

On the west side of Montreal, in the area of Dorval, I found the perfect hiding place for the sub. It was mostly a residential area, but there was a small commercial marina with two old barges tied up together, rusting and gathering layer upon layer of river debris. They had not been moved for a very long time. Between the barges was just enough room for the sub to come up so that the bottom of the hull was flush with the bottoms of the barges, and the portal could stick out of the water a foot and be completely hidden from shore. In fact, the only way you could see the sub was if you climbed onto the barges and peered down into the dark cavity between them, and even then it was difficult to see. It was a great place to hide for a few days, to dry out our things and wait until the river police had given up their search. It also gave me the chance to do what I wanted to do next.

Chapter 27

⁓

SHE CAME OUT OF her house and hurried down the steps. She was carrying a school bag over one shoulder and eating a piece of toast with the other hand. The neighbour's dog came running over and she put the toast in her mouth and stopped to pat the dog. Her school bag fell off her shoulder, she reached for it, dropped her toast and the dog ate it. She stood up and saw me across the street. She wore glasses. I could tell from all the way across the street that the lenses were thick. She was skinny. One sock was higher than the other. I wasn't even sure they were a matching pair. She looked cute but I wondered if maybe my sister was a bit of a nerd.

She started down the sidewalk, stopped, turned and

peered in my direction through her thick glasses, then turned again and headed off to school. I followed. I tried to keep enough distance so she wouldn't think I was following her. I didn't want to scare her. She was small for her age, it seemed to me. She must have been eleven or twelve. Her hair was darker than mine. So was her skin. But I knew it was her. I just knew.

She walked about a mile to school. It took her a lot longer than it should have because she stopped to pat every dog and cat along the way. She even stopped to feed a peanut to a squirrel that seemed to be expecting her. My sister loved animals. That was cool. I wondered if she had any of her own.

The bell had rung already and all the other kids were in school when she arrived. On the way up the steps she dropped her bag for the third time. I couldn't believe it. If there were anything breakable in that bag, it was broken. When she stood up I thought maybe she saw me again. Shoot! Was she going to tell on me? She took a deep breath and sighed. She looked like maybe she was angry. She snorted like a horse, then went inside the school.

My sister lived not far from the river. I had planned to call first, but couldn't think of what to say. Then, I thought maybe I'd just run into her, knowing she'd be going to school. But that wasn't easy either. What was I supposed to say to her? How could I talk to her without scaring her? I was a stranger.

I took Hollie to a park and threw the ball for him. We

must have looked just like any other boy and his dog, not two outlaws wanted by the police. Then we went back to the school and hid behind a tree. I was hoping to see my sister come out for recess. Sure enough, the kids poured out of the school and went into the fenced area at the back. I waited but didn't see her. Where was she? Had she gotten in trouble for being late? I felt like going inside to find out, but couldn't do that. What would I tell them? My sister didn't even know me.

Finally, she came out. She was the last one. She was alone. She crossed the yard alone and sat down alone. She waved to somebody and they waved back. Then she crossed the yard again and sat beside the girl who had waved to her. She pulled a cookie from her bag, broke it in half and gave one half to her friend. Her friend passed her an apple.

Some kids came over. They said something to her. She didn't respond. They said something else and laughed. My sister did not look upset. Suddenly, she turned to them and said something that startled them, and they ran away. The girl beside her laughed. I wondered what my sister had said. I wished I could have gone over and asked, but I would have had to climb the fence, and somebody would probably call the police if I did that. The bell rang and all the kids went back inside. My sister and her friend went last. At the top of the stairs she turned and looked in our direction but I didn't think she saw us. I saw her snort again and go in.

I was waiting when the kids came out for the day. It had been so long since I went to school it was strange to see so many kids pouring out of a building like workers from a factory. It didn't surprise me that my sister was one of the very last. I let her get a head start then followed her.

She went down the street, around a corner and disappeared. When I turned the corner, I didn't see her. Where did she go? I turned around and looked everywhere but couldn't see her. I saw a large billboard. It was a sign advertising fancy women's clothing. Was she hiding behind it? I stepped closer, and then I heard a voice. It was frightened and brave at the same time.

"Here's what's going to happen," she said. "I'm going to scream my head off. Then the police are going to come. Then they're going to arrest you. Then they're going to take you away and throw you in jail. You're going to stay in there until you're very, very old. That's what's going to happen. You'd better run away now while you still have the chance."

Whoa. My sister was tough. "Wait! Don't scream! I'm not going to hurt you. I promise."

"Why are you following me? You've been following me all day."

"Because . . . umm . . . we're related."

She poked her head out from behind the sign. "We're *related*? What are you talking about? I've never even seen you before. How can we be related?"

I took a few deep breaths and stared at her. I was surprised how hard this was and how nervous I was. "I'm your brother."

Her mouth dropped open. Then she shut it, took a step

forward and peered at me through her glasses. "What are you talking about? I don't *have* a brother."

Oh boy, this was weird. "Is your father Russell Pynsent?"

"Yes."

"Then I'm your brother."

She looked confused. "What's your name?"

"Alfred."

"What's your last name?"

"Pynsent."

"What . . . but . . . how do I know you're not just a crazy person who's pretending to be my brother?"

"I'm not a crazy person. But that's a good question. That's what I would ask. Maybe you should call your father and ask him."

"I will."

"A couple of days ago you called him at the dockyard, right?"

"Maybe."

"And it was the third time in a month that you called, right?"

"Actually, it was the fourth. How did you know that?"

"Because I was there when you called."

"Then how come my father never told me about you?"

"Because he doesn't know who I am. Or, he didn't."

"But you just said you were there when I called."

"I was. But I never told him who I was."

"He doesn't know who you are?"

"Maybe he does now, I don't know. He ran away as soon as he saw me."

"Yup. Sounds like Daddy."

Her eyes dropped to the ground. She looked thoughtful. It made her look older. "Why didn't you tell him?"

"I was planning to."

She stared at me again. "This is weird."

"I know."

"How old are you?"

"Sixteen."

"And you're from Newfoundland, right?"

"Yup."

"I never even knew my father was married before."

"My mother died when I was born."

"Really? I'm sorry. That's sad."

"I never knew her."

"I live with my mom."

"Did you ever live with your father?"

"Ummm . . . I think so, but I don't remember. I was really young. He left us and now he lives alone."

"Why do you think he left?"

"Mommy says he's like a hermit. Actually, he's really nice once you get to know him. But it's not easy to do that."

She squinted up her face. "You pretty much have to go to his house. I'm going there this weekend. You should come too. You should definitely come."

"I don't know. I'll think about it. Does he ever call you?"

"Sometimes. But mostly I call him. He doesn't like to talk on the telephone."

"I noticed. So . . . what's your name?"

"My name?"

"Yah. What's your name?"

She stared through her thick lenses. Her eyes were dark, like the river.

"Angel."

Chapter 28

I WAS IN AWE. My sister was the angel of Sheba's dream.

"It's short for Angela. Everybody calls me Angel."

"It's a really nice name."

"Thank you. My mother's going to be home soon."

"Would you like us to walk home with you?"

"Us? Who's us?"

"Oh . . . uhh . . . Hollie and me. He's my second mate."

I tilted my head towards the tool bag. "He's in there."

Angel's eyes opened wide and she came over to the bag and stared in through the mesh. I could feel Hollie's tail wagging.

"You're carrying a *doggie* on your back?"

"Yes, but now that he sees you he wants out."

I pulled the bag over my head, put it down and let Hollie out. He came straight towards Angel, wagging his tail as shyly as a mouse. Angel melted like a snowflake. "He's so *adorable!*"

She looked him over carefully. "What happened to his ears?"

"I don't know. I think maybe some bigger dogs chewed on them."

"Oh my gosh, that's awful! Where did you find him?"

"At sea. Somebody threw him off a wharf. He landed in a boat."

Angel looked wounded but didn't say anything. She stroked Hollie's fur with both hands. "What did you mean by he's your second mate? And what were you doing at sea? Are you a sailor?"

Oh boy. How was I going to explain that?

"Ummm . . . have you ever heard of the Submarine Outlaw, by any chance?"

"Yes. My mom and I watched a show about that on TV once. 'Cause he's from Newfoundland."

"There was a show on TV?"

"Well, I think it was the news. He rescued a family in a storm. And he travels around in his own submarine. And his crew is a seagull and a dog. Isn't that cool?"

"Yah."

"But they can never catch him because he's too clever. I don't know why they want to catch him anyway; he's only doing good things. Have you ever seen him?"

She spoke without looking up at me. She was wrapped up in Hollie.

"Ahhh . . . Angel. That's me."

"What?"

"That's me. I'm the Submarine Outlaw."

She looked up. "No, you're not. Don't be silly."

I just stared at her. I didn't know what else to say.

"You're just making that up. But you're not making up that you're my brother, are you?"

She looked worried.

"I promise you I am your brother. But I really am the Submarine Outlaw too. You don't have to believe me if you don't want to. That doesn't matter. But I *am* your brother, and it matters to me that you believe that."

And then, lo and behold, Seaweed dropped out of the sky and landed on the sidewalk beside Hollie. He glared at Hollie to see if he was eating anything. Seaweed couldn't care less about meeting Angel. But he wanted a dog biscuit.

"Hi, Seaweed."

I took a biscuit out of my pocket and tossed it to him. Then I had to give one to Hollie.

"This is Seaweed. He's my first mate."

Angel stared in disbelief. She took a step forward. Seaweed took a step backward.

"Seaweed doesn't like to be patted. And don't be insulted if he doesn't pay any attention to you. He takes a really long time to warm up to somebody. He's not too fussy about landlubbers anyway. He mostly just likes other seagulls."

"My brother is the Submarine Outlaw. How am I going to tell anybody that? Nobody is going to believe me. Will you come and meet my mom?"

"Sure."

We walked to her house. It took a long time because she stopped to fuss with Hollie so much. Then, she carried him. Seaweed did his cakewalk thing—hopping, jumping and flying in short bursts. He would have made a great vulture.

Angel's mother was waiting on the steps. She stood up when she saw us coming. She was short and skinny too. I wondered what she was going to say.

"Angel?"

"Hi, Mom."

Her mother squinted at me. "Who is that?"

"This is Alfred."

She went to her mother and they hugged. I stayed on the sidewalk.

"And this is Hollie. Isn't he wonderful, Mom?"

"Angel. Who is Alfred?"

Angel gave Hollie a big kiss and hug, then looked into her mother's face.

"My brother."

"Excuse me?"

"He's Daddy's son. From his first wife. Did you know that Daddy had a first wife? And you know what? He's the Submarine Outlaw. He really is. Isn't that amazing?"

Angel's mother's face fell and her arms dropped to her

sides. I could tell from the look on her face that she had not known that Russell Pynsent was married before.

"Yes, I see it right away," she said to me. "And no, dear, I didn't know he was married before. He never told me that."

"He left when I was born," I said. "When my mother died. I never met him till now. But he doesn't know who I am yet, I don't think. Or maybe he knows. I'm not sure."

She looked at me with a frown. "He has a way of leaving, doesn't he?" She put her hands on Angel's head and kissed her again.

Then she looked at Hollie: "Oh, my sweetie, look at you!"

"His name is Hollie, Mommy. Look at his ears. And that's the seagull we saw on TV. Remember? That's the same one!"

Angel pointed to Seaweed, who was standing in the yard looking bored.

"Yes, I remember. Did you bring your submarine to Montreal?"

"Yes."

Angel's eyes opened wide. "You *did*?"

I nodded.

"Oh! Can we see it?"

"Umm . . . I don't know. I promised myself I wouldn't let anybody else in it because it's too dangerous. And, I have to be very careful right now because the police are looking for me."

Her mom looked alarmed. "They're looking for you? Why?"

"Because someone tried to steal my sub. A young guy broke into it, and I had to go in and rescue my crew, and he panicked and almost drowned, and the police came and rescued him. But now they know I'm here in the city with my sub and they probably think I caused the whole incident."

Angel's mom stared at me sympathetically. I could tell that she believed me. "Why don't you come in, Alfred? Come in, please, and have dinner with us. We have lots to talk about."

"Okay. I would like that. Thank you."

"How old are you, Alfred?"

"Sixteen."

"Please come in."

Chapter 29

I STOOD ON THE bridge and watched the police boats scour the river. They were hanging portable sonar devices over their sides. They lowered them into the water the way helicopters did when searching for submarines during military exercises. These were the river police of Montreal. They were searching for me.

It had been two days. I was surprised how determined they were. They motored by the very marina where the sub was, and would have discovered it had they been able to distinguish it from the hulls of the two barges that concealed it. But they couldn't. How lucky that I had chosen that spot, and how lucky that I had stayed a few days with Angel and

Antoinette. Having almost caught me once, the river police must have been very determined to find me again, catch me and arrest me. They might have too, if I had stayed on the move.

As I watched the boats drag their sonar lines like fishermen I wondered how long they would search for me. Would they search upriver and downriver too? Would we have a difficult time returning to sea? How I longed to return to sea. How I longed to sail to the Pacific.

But I would be sorry to leave Angel so soon. In just a few days we had become a family. Maybe it wasn't a regular kind of family, I didn't know, but it was real enough to me. Antoinette was a wonderful mother. She loved Angel more than anything else in the world and would do anything for her. She was wonderful to me too, and seemed happy that Angel had a brother. It would be difficult to leave. But I had to go. I promised Angel I would send her a short-wave radio receiver, so that I could send her messages no matter where I was.

And I promised her something else.

The next day, in the evening, we climbed into Antoinette's car. Angel sat in the back seat. She talked excitedly as we drove across the city. "You will like Daddy, Alfred. It just takes him a while to warm up to someone. He's like Seaweed."

Antoinette drove down a long residential street and stopped in front of an old house.

"I'll wait here," she said. "Take as long as you like; I don't mind. I'll read my book."

Angel and I got out of the car. She took my hand as we went up the front steps of the house and rang the doorbell. I was fighting down my nervousness. There was absolutely nothing to be afraid of, I told myself. But it didn't help much.

The door opened and there he stood, like a man who wished he could run away but had nowhere else to go. His eyes were opened wide. He cleared his throat but didn't say anything.

"Hi Daddy," said Angel. "Can we come in?"

He opened the door wider and made room for us to pass. I couldn't help feeling he was wishing we would just go away. I followed Angel inside.

"Thanks for inviting us over, Daddy."

He followed us into the kitchen where we all sat down at the table. He rubbed his face with his hands. His hands were rough. They weren't as big as Ziegfried's, or my grandfather's, but they were bigger than mine. He looked tired. Angel spoke as if she were talking to one of her friends at school. "We can't stay too long, Daddy. Mommy's waiting in her car. We just wanted to come and say hello. This is Alfred. He's my big brother. He is also the Submarine Outlaw. Did you know that?"

He shook his head. I thought he looked like a caged animal. I didn't know what to say. Suddenly, he opened his mouth. It took a while for the words to come out. "W— would you like a beer?"

I shook my head.

"We would both like a cup of tea," Angel said politely, as if we were sitting in a fancy restaurant.

He got up, went to the sink, filled the kettle with water and put it down on the stove. His movements were slow and deliberate, a little like mine, but slower.

"Alfred is going to send me a special radio, Daddy. Then he can send messages to me when he is travelling around the world. Isn't that neat?"

He nodded and stared at me. I sensed he was going to say something but changed his mind and said something else instead. "How did you become a submariner?"

His question took me by surprise. "Umm . . . I don't know; it's kind of a long story. I had help."

"I figured you'd be a fisherman."

That caught me by surprise too. "No way."

"I bet your grandfather wanted you to."

"He sure did."

He knew my grandfather.

"How is your grandmother?"

"Good. Same as always."

"That's good."

He turned to Angel. Their eyes met and they shared a look. I was starting to understand what she meant by him warming up after a bit. I was feeling less nervous.

"I'll make the tea, Daddy."

"Be careful. The stove is hot."

She smiled. "I know."

"Where are you going next?"

"The Pacific."

"The Pacific Ocean?"

"Yes."

"Can you get there from here?"

I nodded.

"Of course you can, Daddy. Don't you know that all the oceans are connected?"

He looked as if he didn't. I wondered how much schooling he had received but didn't want to ask. Angel did. She would have asked anybody anything.

"How long did you go to school for, Daddy?"

She poured water into the teapot, put the kettle down on the stove and turned off the element. Then, she climbed up onto the counter, reached into the cupboard and brought down three cups.

"Grade eight."

"You and Alfred are the same! He left school at grade eight too. Isn't that interesting?"

We both stared as she dropped two tea bags into the teapot.

"How do you get to the Pacific from here?" he asked.

I wondered if he was asking just to make conversation.

"Umm . . . the best way is to go through the Panama Canal. But I'm not sure if I can do that. My submarine is not legal. But that's only a problem in Canada. In international waters I'm fine, except for coming into port, or sailing through a canal. Then, I need registration papers, which I might be able to get in the Caribbean. I want to go through the canal because it would take forever to sail around the tip of South America, and the north is kind of dangerous."

"You can sail to the Pacific by sailing north?"

He sounded a little interested now.

"Yes. If you sail through the Northwest Passage. It's a maze of islands up in the Arctic. You have to zigzag your way through. But there's a lot of ice, even in summer, although less than there used to be, I guess. Very few sailboats have ever made it through, and usually they've needed an icebreaker to clear a path. But submarines pass through all the time. They sail under the ice. They can do that because they're nuclear powered usually. My sub is diesel-electric, like a World War II sub. But I have a bicycle . . ."

I was going on too much. He was staring at the floor.

"Aren't you afraid?"

"Of what?"

"Of the ice, of the sea, of your submarine breaking down or springing a leak; of drowning, or getting caught and put in jail? Aren't you afraid?"

I didn't know how to answer that. I stared at him. My grandfather's words came to me again. Why did he think my father was not like me? What did he think *I* was like?

"Uhh . . . I guess so. Sometimes."

"You are?"

"Sometimes. Not all the time."

He looked confused. "Then . . . why do you go?"

"I don't know. I guess because I want to so much."

"He's *brave*, Daddy."

He looked as though he were trying to figure me out. We were related. I knew that but still couldn't quite believe it.

"Well, it sounds pretty dangerous."

"It's *exciting*, Daddy, that's what it is. And you know what else? Alfred has a crew, and it's a dog and seagull. Isn't that amazing?"

My crew was waiting for me. Suddenly I felt like leaving. "Maybe we should go, Angel."

"We haven't had our tea yet, silly."

She poured tea into the cups and carried them over to the table one at a time, spilling them a little. He turned and looked at me as if he had just heard a piece of bad news. "I am sorry I wasn't a father to you."

He was shaking a little and I realized he was much more nervous than I was. Angel and I didn't know what to say. I tried hard to think of something. "Nobody's perfect."

"That's right, Daddy. Nobody's perfect. This tea smells good. It's nice that you are having us over for tea, Daddy. Isn't it nice, Alfred?"

"Yes."

She opened the fridge and brought milk and sugar to the table. She poured milk in hers and it spilled over the top. "Ooops! Sorry."

He looked at me and I saw deep sadness in his face. It

looked like it had created the wrinkles there. He wrung his hands together. "When your mother died, I grieved for a long time. I loved her very much. I never saw it coming. She was the picture of health all through the pregnancy."

He stopped, stared at the floor and tried to collect his thoughts. He looked far away. "They wanted me to stay and fish. But I couldn't do that. I hated fishing."

"Me too."

He laughed nervously. "Your grandfather loves fishing."

I grinned. "I know."

"I figured you'd be a fisherman by now for sure."

"No way."

He took a deep breath, then continued. "I stayed for about six months, I guess. One night, I got up and left. I didn't even take anything with me. They were looking after you already, doing everything for you. Every time I looked at you . . ."

He stopped and stared at the floor.

"You must have been very sad, Daddy," Angel said.

"I couldn't stay. There was no work for me. I wouldn't have known how to look after you."

"But why did you never write? Why did you never come back and visit? Why did you run away when you saw me?"

For a moment our eyes met. Then his eyes shut and he dropped his head.

"I was ashamed."

Chapter 30

I TRIED TO IMAGINE my father as a young man. He was leaving Newfoundland because his wife had died. He was burdened with grief. He had a baby but didn't know what to do with it so he left it with its grandparents. Now, as I sat face to face with him, it occurred to me that he hadn't really abandoned me at all. I mean, he hadn't left me in the middle of nowhere, with no one to look after me; he had given me up to people who he knew would love me and look after me better than he could. And they did.

If he *had* taken me, perhaps I would have turned out very differently. Perhaps I would have turned out more like Bim, not knowing what to do with myself, getting into trouble.

Instead, I was given love, care and a good home. Then I met Ziegfried. And then I met Sheba. Now, my life was wonderful. I was happy. I may have been an outlaw but I was happy. I wouldn't change a thing. In a way, my father had done me a favour, as strange as it was to think. It was true. I felt a weight lift off my shoulders, a weight I never even realized I was carrying until that moment.

But Sheba had known.

I took a sip of my tea. I didn't know what else to say. I figured it was time to leave.

"I have three submarines," he said suddenly. "Would you like to see them?"

I had no idea what he was talking about.

"Three *what*, Daddy?"

"Submarines."

"Oh! You mean your models. Oh yes, you should show Alfred your models, Daddy. He will love them. I didn't know you had submarines too."

He got up, went to the next room and clicked on the light. Angel and I followed him. The room was filled from top to bottom with model ships. They were everywhere— on the floor, the walls, window sills, tables, bookshelves, even hanging from the ceiling. I stared in awe. They were beautiful. My father was a ship model artist.

He picked up a submarine. I recognized it immediately. "That's the *Nautilus*," I said.

His face brightened. "You know it?"

"Yah. It was the first nuclear powered sub. It was the first sub to go under the arctic ice to the North Pole."

He looked a little excited now but was pretty good at containing it. He brought the sub over and put it in my hands. It was about three feet long. It was very beautiful. Angel slid her hand under my arm, reached over and touched the side of the sub as if she were patting a cat. "Can I hold it too?"

He looked worried. "Uhhh . . . I don't know. Maybe you'd better not; it's a little heavy."

She made a face. She was disappointed. I watched to see if he would notice her disappointment. Nope. He never saw it. For some reason I couldn't accept that. I didn't know why; it just bugged me. I turned and put the submarine into her arms. "It's not too heavy. You can hold it. Just be careful."

"Be careful," he echoed.

She squinted at him. "Of course I will be careful, Daddy. What do you think I am, clumsy or something?"

I remembered her dropping her school bag. It was a good thing he had never seen that.

"How long have you been making models?"

"Uhh . . . ever since I was seven or eight, I guess."

I looked all around the room. There were ships of all sizes, shapes and types, from destroyers to aircraft carriers to supertankers. There was even a Viking ship with oars. I saw a fishing boat. On its deck was a tiny seagull. "Do you like seagulls?"

"Yes."

That was something else we had in common. "Have you ever been to sea?"

"No."

I could guess why. For a moment I wished I could take him to sea and show him what it was like. But this was not the time. Maybe there would be another time. I hoped so. I turned to Angel. "We probably should go. Your mom is waiting."

She frowned and handed the sub back to him. We went out and he followed us to the door. He looked sad. "Will you come back and visit me again?"

I would. I knew I would. "Yes."

"Of course we will, Daddy. Of course we will."

She wrapped her arms around him and hugged him. He looked like there was something he wanted to say but couldn't get the words out. He stuck out his hand and I took it. Our eyes met for the second time. "I have something I want to give you," he said.

He went back inside. Angel and I stood at the door and waited. I was glad we had come.

He came back with a small envelope. "I want you to have this."

He stared at the envelope and shook as he passed it to me. He took my hand again. "I am sorry I let you down," he said.

"You didn't . . ." Angel started, but I interrupted her.

"You didn't let me down. I have a wonderful life."

His eyes welled up. I shook his hand and bit my lip.

"Will you write me?" he asked.

"I will. I promise."

Then I let go and took Angel's hand and we went out the door. Her mother was waiting. I saw her look up from her book and smile at us. She had waited so patiently. She was a wonderful mother. If my mother were alive, I figured she would have been just like that.

She would have. I knew it.

I sat in the back seat this time and Angel sat in the front. As the car pulled out, she turned around and leaned over the seat. "What did he give you?"

"I don't know."

"Are you going to open it?"

"I guess so."

The envelope was old and thin. It was sealed with tape. I had to tear it open.

"What is it?"

"A picture."

Inside was a photograph. I held it up and stared at it. Two people were standing in front of an apple tree. A man and a woman. The tree was full of apple blossoms. She was wearing a bright yellow dress and her hair was long and dark. He was wearing a brown suit. She was smiling and bursting with energy, you could see it on her face. He was shy and awkward, but you could tell that he was in love with her. It reminded me of Ziegfried and Sheba. It was a happy day.

"What is it?"

"A picture of my mother and father."

"Can I see it?"

I passed it to her. I saw Antoinette take a quick peek at it. Then she reached back and squeezed my hand. I looked out the window.

"She's pretty," Angel said.

I thought so too.

Epilogue

SHEBA'S COVE WAS shrouded in darkness when we sailed in. The moon and stars were wrapped in fog. I knew her cove so well I could tell exactly where we were just by the feel of the sub. When I opened the hatch, Seaweed burst out like a bat. Hollie and I climbed out, jumped onto the rock, stood up and breathed in the island air. The air of Sheba's island had a unique smell, a very pleasant mix of fog, wood smoke, sweet flowers, goats and spices. How I longed to sail to the places where those spices grew. And I would, very soon now.

It was the middle of the night. I didn't know if we could sneak inside without waking her. Sheba was a light sleeper. I crept up the rock as silently as I could. Hollie crept behind me, keeping an exact distance and stopping when I stopped. He was pretty sneaky when he wanted to be. Seaweed stayed by the sub.

The kitchen light was on. Maybe she was up. Or maybe she had been leaving the light on for me. It was a gentle blue light. Maybe she was raising new tomato plants in the kitchen. I took in the outline of the cottage at a glance. There were enough animals here to start a farm. There was enough love here to heal the world, it seemed to me. It was a haven of love. It was a sanctuary.

I crept up to the window and peered in. She wasn't there. She must have been sleeping. The cockatiels were lined up on a wire above the stove, their bellies shaking with each breath. Edgar, the kitchen goat, was curled up like a dog beside the wood box. Marmalade, the cat, was sleeping on top of him. Sheba's book of flowers was open on the table. She had been reading. A large pot was sitting on the counter. She must have been soaking beans. That meant she was expecting Ziegfried. I hoped so. I felt a deep happiness to be back.

Ziegfried had been right; it had only taken a month. Sheba had been right too; I had survived and come back richer than before. Much richer. Discovering Angel was the greatest treasure I could find, greater than all the treasures I would ever find beneath the sea. Meeting my father gave me a better sense of who I was and where I had come from. I needed time to think about everything he had said but I already felt that I liked him and wanted to get to know him.

I would write. I would take the time to think of exactly what I wanted to say, and then I would write it all down in a letter and mail it to him. And when I came back from the Pacific, I would visit him again, and Angel and Antoinette: my new family.

As I stood and stared at the magical cottage, wondering if I should try to sneak in without waking Sheba, or return to the sub till morning, I felt a hand come down upon my shoulder. I nearly jumped out of my skin.

"Alfred?"

I turned to see the towering figure behind me. Her warm, loving arms wrapped around me and pulled me tight. I should have known. You don't sneak up on an oracle.

ACKNOWLEDGEMENTS

I would like to thank the many wonderful students and readers I have met in schools and libraries, especially those who have taken the time to write to me. Your response to these books is invaluable to me and greatly appreciated.

Invariably, I arrive at the doorstep of Ron and Veronica Hatch with a sack on my back filled with phrases, images and fragments of a storyline going someplace. I always leave with a polished novel in hand. It is an elevating experience and I am grateful.

I wish to thank the incomparable Julia, Peter and Thomas, the most important people in my life, who are boldly setting about to make the world a better place to be and are constantly inspiring me with their example. I also wish to thank my dearest friends: Chris, Natasha and Chiara, whose home and friendship is my secret haven; and the lovely and nature-loving Diana, Maria and Sammy; my dear and dedicated friend, Zaan, creating great works of art on the other side of the world; and my inspired and joyful buddy, Hugh. All of these people keep me on a path straight and true.

As always, I must express my deepest gratitude to my mother Ellen, my first reader and first inspiration, for her tireless love and support. I also wish to thank sweet Dale for bringing such joy and happiness into my life. And thanks to the young and intrepid Jake, for his kindness, wisdom and courage.

Finally I wish to recognize the support of the Province of Nova Scotia through the Department of Tourism, Culture & Heritage.

ABOUT THE AUTHOR

 Raised beside the sea in Antigonish, Nova Scotia, Philip Roy celebrates the sea in most of his stories. He also loves submarines. The Submarine Outlaw series grew out of a combination of those interests and his joy of travelling around the world. Educated in music and history, with a healthy dose of the classics, especially those great epics of old, he strives to create entertaining and enlightening stories in the modern day that sit on top of classical themes like a ship upon a vast ocean. These stories now bring him into the classroom where he enjoys meeting the bright stars of the next generation. Just so, his experience of being a writer has become richer many times over. Philip is now busy working on *Tales of the Pacific*, book four of the Submarine Outlaw series.

Recycled
Supporting responsible use
of forest resources
www.fsc.org Cert no. SGS-COC-003153
© 1996 Forest Stewardship Council
FSC

MARQUIS

Marquis Book Printing Inc.

Québec, Canada
2010

Printed on Silva Enviro 100% post-consumer EcoLogo certified paper,
processed chlorine free and manufactured using biogas energy.